HARVEST OF TERROR

Adela Gale

Curley Publishing, Inc.

South Yarmouth, Ma.

Library of Congress Cataloging-in-Publication Data

Gale, Adela.
   Harvest of terror / Adela Gale.—Large print ed.
     p. cm.
   1. Large type books. I. Title.
   [PS3557.A41145H37   1991]
   813'.54—dc20
   ISBN 0–7927–0725–7 (large print)   90–42467
   ISBN 0–7927–0726–5 (pbk.)   CIP

Published in Large Print by arrangement with Donald MacCampbell, Inc. in the United States, Canada, the U.K. and British Commonwealth and the rest of the world market.

Distributed in Great Britain, Ireland and the Commonwealth by CHIVERS LIBRARY SERVICES LIMITED, Bath BA1 3HB, England.

Printed in Great Britain

HARVEST OF TERROR

ONE

Had I been a philosopher or a metaphysician, instead of a private-duty nurse, I might have given some thought on that triumphant winter morning to the laws of balance that govern the universe. I might have considered that the windfall of joy and success that had swept into my uneventful existence that day would be weighed down on my life's scale by an equal measure of dismal events.

That the compensating misfortunes would evoke more terror than grief I could not have foreseen, but the idea drifted through my mind only to the extent that I thought, "Everything that has happened to me this morning is too wonderful to be true!"

How can I begin to describe the three occurrences that touched an icy, windswept February day in New York with the heartwarming promise of springtime? These events were not isolated; they were inextricably woven together into the fabric of my life, one answering a prayer, another fulfilling a need, and the third bringing about the realization of a dream. Let me begin with the prayer, for this is where it all began.

I had always felt a deep personalized compassion for patients entrusted to my care. Perhaps because my own childhood had been so unbearably lonely, I had developed a deep appreciation for the value of ... how shall I express it? Of *caring*. Of knowing that someone cares enough to provide not merely necessities and even physical comforts (for I had never lacked either in the smartly furnished, efficiently managed apartment that had been my companionless cage as a child), but that barely definable extra quality that exists between one human being and another, which for lack of a more specific definition, I must label love.

My parents had not been inordinately wealthy, but they had both succeeded at their separate careers. My father served in some quasi-administrative capacity in the New York transit system; I never knew exactly what he did because the rare communication between us was confined to polite, only vaguely interested inquiries about my health and my schoolwork. My mother, from whom I had inherited, for better or worse, all my physical characteristics, was the sportswear buyer for a chain of women's wear shops that advertised "high fashion at low prices."

Engrossed in the challenging, often dog-eat-dog competition of the retail business, my mother had little time to spare for my father, and still less, it seemed, for me. She maintained that a successful executive organized everything so efficiently that his, or her, physical presence became superfluous. Certainly her office operated smoothly during her frequent trips to check on merchandising operations of the chain's out-of-state stores; our apartment home, streamlined to avoid clutter, and under the supervision of an ever-changing string of colorless housekeepers, was managed in the same way.

On the two or three evenings of the week when neither of my parents were being wined and dined by dress manufacturers or politicians, and they had dinner at home, it was always *after* I had been fed and tucked away for the night by one of the aseptic and taciturn Aggies or Bessies who were hired to look after me. Even in later years, when I was allowed to share their dinner hour, I sensed that my parents included me in their conversation self-consciously. When their talk swerved from their current job tribulations, I sensed that it was done out of that same sense of guilt that drove them, periodically, to present me with expensive, unimaginative gifts.

No child who yearned for noisy, hopefully muddy, companionship with other children, ever had a larger collection of untouched stuffed toy animals; I ached for a tiny show of love, and I was given another monstrously huge panda bear or giraffe. Unlike most children, I loved school, for it was during the hours that I spent at the "highly recommended" private institution my mother had selected for me that I got to play with other youngsters. I have only dim memories of those important contacts, for all my friendships were short-lived. Day students came and went, their attendance dictated by the fluctuating incomes and shifting careers of their parents. After school, instead of walking home together through familiar side streets to a single familiar neighborhood, we dispersed in cars and taxis, or in the care of walking substitute "mothers" who had arrived, by clockwork, at exactly the moment we were dismissed.

No other children lived in the apartment building, and my overprotective parents made certain that I was not exposed to the dangers of the street or the park. My mother had been thirty years old when I was born; if my arrival interfered with her career, she buried her resentment enough to make certain that nothing "unpleasant" happened to me. As a result, I was probably the world's youngest virtual hermit.

I filled the empty hours with reading (always romantic, adventurous fiction) and constructing fantasies that (quite literally, after I had read Washington Irving's *Tales of the Alhambra*) carried me off to castles in Spain.

Thinking back now to those enchanted Moorish castles of my childish imagination – my escapes from the hermetically sealed rooms that served as my home – I can understand the irresistible lure of Castillo de los Tres Gatos – the Castle of the Three Cats – to which I traveled with naive hope that a romantic daydream must be coming true, and in which I learned that one does not sleep through all nightmares; sometimes, one is forced to live through them.

In retrospect, I understand, too, the clammy horror that seized me at the sight of two dead kittens that were to play so significant a role in the nightmare at Castillo de los Tres Gatos. I recall a pleading, eight-year-old child's request: *"Mama, couldn't I have a kitty? A real kitty to play with?"*

"Terry, darling, we can't have animals in an apartment. Animals are so . . . messy!"

My mother's crisp, yet charmingly persuasive executive's voice! Along with the voice, I remember a heart-shaped face dominated by wide, dark-fringed eyes of a shade that poetic souls have called cornflower blue, a beautifully manicured hand giving a nervous pat to a gleaming black, intricate coiffure. Except that my own black hair is combed straight, to turn up only slightly at the jawline, the face that I looked into so beseechingly is the face that my mirror reflects back to me today.

"*I'd teach it to be nice, Mama. It could sleep in a little box next to my bed, and I could . . .*"

"*Terry, please! You have all your lovely toys and games.*"

"*But they don't PLAY with me! Please, Mama?*"

"*We'll see, dear. Right now, I have to call the office. Elkhart's absolutely screaming for that new Glen plaid jacket, and we can't get delivery unless I . . .*"

She was on her way to the telephone, leaving me clinging to the ephemeral hope of "We'll see." Two days later, my mother came home with a surprise. "An adorable, soft, fluffy white kitten," she said as she handed me the ribbon-tied package. Even before I tore off the familiar wrapping paper from the toy store, I knew that the "fluffy white kitten" would be a rigid, glass-eyed thing with fake fur and a pink felt tongue. Late that evening, after my mother had gone back to her office to get a shipping emergency under

6

control, I took out my raging frustration on that hateful, sanitary, lifeless toy, cutting the belly open with manicure scissors and scattering its cotton stuffing over the floor of my room.

Our current housekeeper cleaned up the only mess created by that disappointing pet. My mother never knew that I had destroyed it; how could she miss one stuffed toy in an imposing gallery she rarely visited? Yet it was one of the incidents I remembered with regret twelve years later, on the eve of my graduation from a nursing school in Chicago.

My father had died of a liver ailment the year before, but I had hoped my mother would be present to see me receive my cap and R.N. pin. Ironically, the wreckage of the plane in which she had died a fiery death was found just west of Chicago. My mother had not had time to stop for my graduation; she had been on a buying trip to California when the crash occurred.

I was not bitter, nor was I inconsolably grief-stricken; by then, we had been strangers too long for the excruciating pain of final loss. It was the love my parents had never claimed, a love that ached to be given to someone, that I lavished on my patients, and, later, after I had returned to New York, on Craig Addison.

It was easy to love Dr. Addison's teen-aged

patient – easier still to fall in love with the physician himself. For two months, serving as Denise Westlake's special-duty nurse on the seven-to-three shift, I had shared the doctor's agonized bewilderment. Faced by a mysterious ailment that threatened the delicate auburn-haired girl's life, Craig Addison exhausted himself in the search for a clue to Denise's raging fever. And only two weeks before, following a persistent hunch, the doctor had ordered one more X ray and found the source of the potential killer.

One week of intensified doses of antibiotics. One week during which I prayed, not only because I had grown extremely fond of our pretty little seventeen-year-old patient, but because I knew how desperately Craig Addison wanted to save her. Then came that glorious February morning, when Craig Addison bounded into the tiny supply room where I was gathering fresh linens for Denise's bed, burst into the shelf-lined cubicle like an irrepressible adolescent, when always before I had seen him only as a broodingly serious, conservative, and impersonal physician.

His wide grin belied the tiring ordeal that was now behind him. "I wanted you to be the first to know, Miss Reed. I'm signing Denise out tomorrow!"

I don't remember what I said; probably

something about how wonderful it had been to see Denise smiling when I walked into her room at seven that morning. My words were lost in a sudden, totally unexpected embrace. Even more astounding than being swept into Craig's arms was the warm, brief pressure of his lips against mine.

He released me almost as abruptly, his usually somber brown eyes alight with laughter. "That's for never doubting we'd pull her through," he said. "Remember? After the fifth X ray practically ruled out osteomyelitis, and I'd ruled out every other possibility myself?"

I was too breathless to do anything but nod. Craig was telling me that the kiss had been nothing more personal than an exuberant reaction to his triumph. That, and a thanks for having believed, even when Denise seemed to be slipping away from us, that somehow, in some way, her doctor would solve the deadly puzzle that had stumped a veritable army of consulting specialists. It didn't matter. He had never called me by my given name; never, I was certain, seen me as anything but a devoted member of a medical team. And now he had kissed me. Impulsively, unmindfully, unromantically, perhaps. But he had kissed me. I was barely aware of anything else.

"My mind kept coming back to that fall

she'd had, ice-skating," Craig was saying. "The infection *had* to be in a bone, but no erosion showed up on film. We'd run every test, considered every possibility . . . a septic lesion in the brain, meningitis . . . every possibility. But there was the enlarged heart. That blunted apex kept pointing to a staph infection that had developed into osteo. Blood cultures grew staph aureus in the lab." One of Craig's hands ran over his light brown, closely clipped hair. The handsome face was lined now by a rueful smile. "Ironic. The very antibiotics we were using to fight symptoms were suppressing the infection just enough to confuse an accurate diagnosis. But the dosage wasn't massive enough to combat a type eighty staph. And meanwhile we had the infection spreading to a heart valve, pumping the virus all through her system."

I mumbled something about having overheard several attending doctors at the nurses' station earlier; they had been lauding the painstaking medical detective work that had produced a diagnosis.

"I couldn't give up," Craig Addison said. "Not just because Walter Westlake and I are close personal friends, or because I've known Denise since . . . oh, since her mother died, when she was just a little girl. It was . . ."

He stopped, and I knew that he would

10

never be able to explain his dogged tenacity in words. He had battled for Denise's cure because she was a human being and he was a doctor. It was as simple as that, yet Craig was too self-effacing to paint himself as an exceptionally dedicated healer. His sixth sense had produced a miracle, but had it proven wrong, he would have gone on fighting against time and the odds that favored death.

How inevitable it had been that I should fall in love with this man. Other nurses at the hospital had raved about his height and physique, his handsome features, his calm, deep voice. These were secondary assets, nice but less important to me than his keen intelligence and a shared compassion – they had won my heart. And my love had grown without the faintest hope, for hospital grapevine had warned me that Dr. Addison, at thirty-two, was determined to avoid romantic entanglements.

I had heard only enough of the rumors to know that he was a widower – that his wife had drowned with a male companion in a boating accident off Long Island. The circumstances had added bitterness to the young doctor's shock; Mrs. Addison had been aboard the yacht of one of Craig's best friends, a prominent attorney. The friend's wife had thought her husband was out of town on

11

business; Craig had seen his wife off on a "visit to her sister in Canada." No one at the hospital knew more than that, except for the fact that Dr. Addison never dated, and treated even the most attractive nurses with casual indifference.

I had no right to be encouraged by that impetuous, brotherly kiss. Yet I was soaring on a romantic cloud when I heard Craig say, "Denise is going to do her recuperating in Majorca, from what her father tells me."

"Majorca?" For all I knew, he was referring to a health resort in Florida.

Craig smiled at my bewildered expression. "It's an island, off the coast of Spain."

"Oh." I felt my cheeks burning under the amused stare. "I suppose Mr. Westlake –"

"He won't be going," I was told. "Walter can't tear himself away from that advertising agency of his. Since he lost his wife, Denise and his business have become his whole life." There was an embarrassing pause; perhaps Craig had been reminded that he, too, had buried his aloneness in work. Then, hurriedly, he said, "I'd better tell you this, Miss Reed. Walter Westlake has had two heart attacks, and there's nothing I can do to induce him to quit. He knows he's going to drive himself into the grave, but he insists he'd die even sooner if he gave up running his agency."

12

"But if he's so crazy about Denise . . ."

"The way he puts it, he doesn't want Denise around when . . ." Craig shook his head slowly from side to side. "Well, he says he wants to spare her the shock of his death. I'm still going to try to convince him that he'd add ten years to his life if he retired now and went to Majorca with Denise. He has money enough, heaven knows. But . . . I don't know. He has a brother and sister-in-law living on the island. Apparently he has some idea about getting Denise established in as he says, 'a permanent homelike atmosphere,' before he dies. Try arguing with a stubborn, self-made success like Westlake!"

"Somebody *should*," I said. "I'd like to, though it's none of my business. And there won't be any chance to, if Denise is going home tomorrow."

"Oh, she's still going to need nursing care," Craig said quickly. "At home for a month and then for a few more months abroad." The look of wry amusement had crept into his eyes once more. "I don't suppose you have any question in your mind about which nurse Denise wants to have around? She's very fond of you, Miss Reed. Her father knows you've gone far beyond the call of duty in caring for her, keeping her morale up. It wasn't even necessary for me to recommend you for the

13

job. You should enjoy Majorca. I'm told it's a beautiful place."

A prayer, a wish, a dream! Denise was well again, Craig had kissed me, I was going to a romantic island off the Spanish coast! It was as though the icy streets of New York had suddenly thawed under an April sun.

It was not until I had talked with Denise's father that afternoon, promising that gray-eyed dynamo that I would accept the assignment . . . not until then that a dismal thought clouded my new-found joy. If Craig Addison had encouraged Mr. Westlake to hire me, he had not been concerned with the fact that I would be leaving the country in a few weeks. There was only the remotest possibility that I would care for another of his patients; more probably, we would never see each other again. That kiss had meant no more than a pat on the back for a job well done.

It was with mixed feelings that I projected myself into the weeks ahead – the prospect of a trip to the faraway land of my childhood dreams clouded by the shattering of a flickering hope. Between the excitement and the disappointment, there was no room for a third reaction. Yet, had I been able to peer more closely at the future, both emotions would have given way to an overpowering fear.

But, then, I had no way of foreseeing the terror that waited for me in a castle that was so horribly unlike my little-girl castles in Spain.

TWO

It was a mistake to think that I would never see Craig Addison again. I saw him on numerous occasions during the weeks I spent at the Westlake's fashionable home on Long Island. But even in the warm, convivial atmosphere created by Walter Westlake and his amazingly unspoiled daughter, even in this setting, where I was regarded as a member of the family rather than an employee, Craig maintained the formalized doctor-nurse relationship that had been established at the hospital. It seemed unbelievable that he had once clasped me close to him.

To spare myself additional pain, I made up my mind to face reality and to crowd him from my thoughts. I concentrated, instead, on building up the health of my young patient who, by then, was also a dear friend.

Denise rewarded me by dutifully following the regimen set down by her doctor. There had been no crippling aftereffects from her illness, and her heart was pronounced undamaged. She had emerged from her ordeal weakened and underweight, but there was no indication that, after a period of rest, she would not be able to resume her normal active life.

How amazing it was, I thought, that this elfin-pretty girl had managed to grow up without the scars that had afflicted me at the same age. Denise, too, had been left in the care of often-indifferent housekeepers. Her father was enamored of his work, devoting to the advertising agency he had built up, as he phrased it, "from scratch," the majority of his waking hours. And because there was plenty of money, there was no reason to doubt that Mr. Westlake had often substituted expensive gifts for his presence. Yet Denise was the embodiment of happy, well-adjusted, enthusiastic youth.

Like her father, she had distinctive, penetrating gray eyes. Also like him, she laughed often and honestly. From Walter Westlake she had acquired a talent for making people like her instantly, though she was as frank in her denunciations as he was, and as stubborn in her opinions. They were both generous to a fault, both possessed of an almost manic enthusiasm for whatever attracted their interest.

It delighted me to see them together, he with his lunch-hour-health-club tan, his silvery hair and trim moustache, and Denise with her pale, almost translucent skin and her luxuriant crop of shoulder-length hair gleaming with red-gold highlights. These minor differences in coloring paled before the similarity of their uniquely shaded eyes, and before personalities that might have been cast in the same mold. Was this why they were so close to each other? I wondered. Was this why Denise had never felt shunted aside, and why, although she urged her father to accompany her to Majorca, she never doubted his love for her when he refused to go?

By the time they were packed, and all the travel arrangements had been made, I understood. Walter Westlake might have deprived Denise of his time, but in the moments they *did* share, his love for her was so obvious that it was an almost palpable reality. Denise had always known that she was loved; the knowledge had left her secure and free to make countless friends, to pursue a myriad of interests. It was from these two that I learned that time does not govern the quality of love.

Furthermore, Walter Westlake's plan for his daughter was a sincere expression of his love. "Denise understands why I can't quit working," he told me one evening. "Until she's ready for college, she'll be better off with my brother and his wife." He paused to light another in a steady chain of cigarettes. "Durward's a little unsociable – all wrapped up in some crackpot research work, but Denise's Aunt Ilse lives for fun. Lot more wholesome atmosphere for a kid than rattling around in this big house with only me for a family."

He said nothing about the possible heart attack for which his hectic business activity was preparing him, and I didn't pry into his personal life. Strangely, with his artificial tan and his general well-fed aspect, he looked like the last man in the world to be sending his daughter overseas to spare her the shock of his imminent demise. I thought of that irony often in the weeks to come. His primary concern was with his child's happiness; yet how blindly, in trying to protect Denise, he exposed her to a fate which, even now, I shudder to recall.

THREE

The trans-Atlantic flight lay behind us. There had been only a momentary view of the Spanish heartland before another plane whisked us off from Madrid toward the Balearic Islands in the Mediterranean, and Denise, who had made the trip two years earlier with her father, bubbled with the enthusiasm of a new tourist guide.

"I loved Majorca, but old-time residents complain that it's changed," Denise said. "People like my Uncle Durward and Aunt Ilse. They remember when it was a bargain paradise for artists and writers. Talking about writers ... my uncle's working on a book, did you know?" Denise giggled suddenly, her fresh blooming color and laughing eyes a gratifying sight to one who had stood over her bed hoping she would survive one more night. "It took me two months to memorize the title. *Aspects of Herbology and Mycology in Relation to Medieval Witchcraft Practices in Central and Southern Europe.* Isn't that a riot? He's been working on the book for eight years, and Daddy says there can't be more than five people in the world who'll want to

19

read it. *If* Durward ever gets it finished. And *if* anybody publishes it."

"You'd have to be well off to be able to devote that much time to a project," I observed.

Denise shook her head. "Nope. You'd just have to have a generous brother who owns a big ad agency. Uncle Durward's a scholar, but he hates teaching. And he's flopped at just about every business Daddy tried to set up for him. I guess he's an expert in his subject. It makes it kind of rough on his wife, though. Ilse is a doll. She loves people and parties and . . ." Denise shrugged. "She was brought up with scads of money. In Vienna, I think. Then her family lost everything during the Second World War, and now she has to struggle along with a monthly check from her brother-in-law, and put up with a kooky husband who won't come out of his hothouse to take her to parties. I don't know what makes her so sweet and patient. I'd be miserable."

"And they've lived in Majorca for a long time?" I asked.

"Oh, ages," Denise told me. "They both remember Palma – that's the capital city – when it wasn't crawling with tourists, especially during the season. I guess prices have gone up now that Palma isn't a hideaway town anymore. Lots of the really colorful people have moved out to the villages, or to the other islands; Minorca or Iviza. Gosh, there's almost hourly plane service from Barcelona now, and direct service from every capital in Europe. The joint really jumps."

I remembered talk of a mountainside castle, overlooking a tiny seaside village. "But your relatives don't live in the city, do they?"

"No, they're way out in the toolies." Denise turned on her impish grin. "A person like my aunt ought to live in Paris, but Ilse just adores that old place. She likes to entertain people from the expatriate colony, and it's kind of glamorous to be able to tell them the place is haunted."

It was my turn to smile. "Oh, really?"

"That's what they *say*." Denise made a disbelieving gesture. "The way I heard it, the place belonged to some Spanish nobleman or knight or . . . I don't know what. Anyway, he was insanely jealous of his wife, but he was always leaving her to go fight wars or something on the mainland. Most of the time she was alone in the creepy castle with just an army of servants and three pet cats."

"That's why it's called Castillo de los Tres Gatos?"

Denise nodded. "I guess. *Well.* One day this count, or whatever, came back after he'd

21

been gone for a long time, and it seems there was a servant who hated the lady of the house because she'd caught him stealing or something. And this character gave the master of the house a lot of malarkey about how his wife had been unfaithful."

"Sort of an Iberian Iago type," I said.

Denise, who had probably been too busy having fun during Shakespeare season at her high school, frowned uncomprehendingly. "Could be," she said. "All *I* know is that this nut didn't even give his wife a chance to explain. He stabbed her with a sword and cemented her body up in a wall. Isn't that gruesome? Only, her pet cats sneaked in to be next to her, and they got sealed in between the walls alive. So they yowled and the guy got caught and I think he was hanged or something like that."

"I suppose the cats are heard wailing at night?" I asked. (I decided not to ask Denise if she had ever read a similar tale by Edgar Allen Poe.) "That's the usual bit."

"Oh, sure," Denise said. "That is, people *say* they do. And the lady's ghost is supposed to walk around in her favorite gardens at night, trailing blood from her stab wound. *I* never saw her, but Ilse says she can't keep servants because they're all so superstitious." Denise tossed her auburn hair and released

22

another of her musical giggles. "If you ask me, my poor aunt uses that as an excuse whenever the help quits. She doesn't want her friends to know she spent all her money on parties, or else Uncle Durward blew it on rare books, so they couldn't pay the cook or the maids. I'd quit, too, if I didn't get paid for months at a time."

I was beginning to get a candid seventeen-year-old's view of the "secure household" her father had chosen for her. The Majorca branch of the Westlake family might not be financially stable, I decided, but at least they weren't foolish enough to be troubled by imaginary spectral visitors. Neither was Denise, and I complimented her good sense. "You had me worried for a moment. I remember hearing you ask your father if 'that horrible woman' would still be at your uncle's home."

Denise reflected for a moment, trying to recall the conversation. Then, apparently remembering, she shrieked her amusement. "Oh, *that* horrible woman! I meant Anita Alma. She's no ghost. She's disgustingly real."

"Anita Alma," I repeated. "That sounds like a name somebody made up."

"It *is*." Denise assured me. "Everything about that phoney is made up. Her hair, her

23

eyes, her personality."

As our plane droned toward Majorca, I learned that Anita Alma had been a houseguest at the castle during that brief visit paid by Denise and Walter Westlake. According to Denise, she had been an untalented Continental actress, whose brief success had rested more on her amorous affairs than on her ability. Now in her forties and penniless, she was obsessed by a need to find a husband before her fading beauty deserted her completely.

"My aunt collects characters like that," Denise sighed. "Ilse thinks they're glamorous, like ghosts. Personally, I'll take the lady with the wailing cats over a spook like Alma."

I had never before heard a derogatory word about anyone from my patient, and her intense dislike of Anita Alma had a disquieting effect upon me. Those lines of hatred didn't belong on Denise's pretty young face, and I wondered what could have inspired them. I didn't have to ask.

"Anita took one look at Daddy and went right to work. You can imagine how he looked to a fading bag who digs furs and jewelry. I mean, here was an attractive widower with a successful business in America. Wow!" For a few seconds Denise stared down at the changing green landscape far below us, her eyes narrowed in contempt. Then, with more venom than I would have thought possible from her, she said, "Anita made such an idiot of herself, chasing my father – he practically laughed in her face. I guess she decided he gave her the cold shoulder because of me. Stupid! I didn't have to tell him I'd leave home if he ever married somebody like that. But *she* thought I was to blame. Anita left before we did, so mad she didn't even say goodbye. I'm sure I won't see her again. But, oh, man, did she despise *me!* Oh, look, there's the sea! Look, Terry, that's the Mediterranean! Isn't that the most gorgeous blue you ever saw?"

Denise's resentful mood was exploded by a more typical exuberance. We were nearing our destination; minutes later the sparkling sapphire sea was studded by a group of incredibly green islands, and shortly afterward we were taxiing across the Palma International Airport in Majorca.

Strangely, I had experienced no foreboding sensations during our discussion of ghosts, or even during Denise's icy disparagement of that pathetic woman with the obviously theatrical name. Perhaps it was because, during those discussions, the sun had been shining, rimming the fleecy clouds around us with an iridescent glow of gold. As we set foot

25

on the soil of Majorca, abruptly, inexplicably, it began to drizzle.

Was it only the pall of gray that had blotted out the sun, or was it some innate sixth sense that filled me with a sudden totally unexplainable dread? Looking back, I am certain that the disappointing, clamminess of the weather would not have affected me; I was too excited about my first flight, my first visit to a foreign land, to be depressed by mere weather. I did not, then, have strong beliefs in precognition, premonition, second sight – call it what you will. I am still skeptical about the validity of intuitive feelings, and would not claim that some vague, not understood power warned me to turn back. In any case, it would have been impossible to disrupt my patient's plans because of a visceral hunch. All I know is that during that clammy interval after we got off the plane, if I had followed my almost overpowering instincts, Denise and I would have been spared the horror of Castillo de los Tres Gatos.

FOUR

If the sun had been shining, the pastel, red-tile-roofed houses of San Ysidro would have resembled gay children's blocks tumbling down the hillside toward a crayon-blue sea.

In spite of the shroud of gray that enveloped the village that afternoon, I found it as lovely and fanciful as a storybook illustration. Colorful sails of tiny fishing vessels dotted the miniature bay; brightly painted donkey carts, like the boats and houses, resembled whimsical toys. And the villagers, seemingly oblivious to the drizzle, added their quaint charm and color to an extravagant array of brilliant flowers.

It would be breathtaking when the sun emerged, I knew. Now, as Denise and I wound through the village in a chauffeur-driven car that had been sent to the airport to meet us, my earlier apprehensive mood gave way to one of eager anticipation; how foolish it had been to construct fearful visions about a place that managed to look cheerful and bright even under a dismal sky.

As we climbed upward, inland from the village, Denise craned forward, waiting for

27

the castle to come into view. "If you think the weather's gloomy wait'll you see where we're going to be staying," she said with a grin. "If my aunt and uncle weren't so crazy about flowers, you could call it one big blob of gray. Wait a second . . . around this next turn, I think."

Her guess had been wrong. The car was piloted around several more corkscrew bends in the steep road before Castillo de los Tres Gatos came into view. But Denise had been correct in describing it; devoid of the towers, moats, and intricate balustrades I had always associated with castles, the building we approached was a mammoth, three-story, gray-stone rectangle, its forbidding, exterior broken only by a row of black wrought-iron balconies protruding from the second floor.

I would have been disappointed, except for the profusion of trees and flowers that managed to keep this imposing and austere structure from jutting up from the hill's summit like a monstrous stone crypt. Masses of purple-red bougainvillea climbed the walls, and as we came to a stop at the end of a gravel driveway lined with yellow blossoming trees, I noticed a short, stocky man, his dress strangely unlike that of the workmen we had seen in the village below, hoeing weeds from a rose bed at the side of the building. The castle, with its tiny Gothic windows and black-framed balconies was, indeed, saved from cold ugliness by a gardener's devotion.

As our chauffeur stopped the car before a tiled terrace that ran the breadth of the building, I leaned forward to address him in my meager high school Spanish.

"Por favor traije los valises . . ."

Denise's excited laughter interrupted me as she opened her door. "I forgot to tell you, Terry. He doesn't speak Spanish."

My bewildered expression must have matched that of our driver. "He doesn't . . ."

"They speak Catalan here." Without waiting for any help from me, and amazingly energetic considering her recent illness, Denise called back, "Dad says if you learn French, Rumanian, and Italian, and then throw in a little German plus a few American Indian languages, in about ten years you'll know how to say good morning in Catalan. Come on, Terry. He'll bring the luggage. I want to see what happened to the welcoming committee."

I was hurrying across the terrace to catch up with my exuberant patient when her question was at least partially answered. As the dark, ornately carved door swung open, the sound of its creaking hinges was accompanied by a delighted cry: "Denise! Oh, how wonderful!

My poor baby . . . I have been so worried!"

The voice, with its faint German accent, belonged to a short, plumpish woman who appeared to be in her late thirties. As she ran forward to embrace Denise, I guessed that she was one of those chubby-petite women who invariably look as though they were dressed for a garden party. She wore a floral print chiffon dress embellished by a pearl necklace and pearl button earrings that contrived to emphasize the baby roundness of her face, and her ash-blond hair was piled high in an elaborate coiffure that involved every trick of the hairdresser's art.

Her tearful but joyous welcome to Denise dispelled the gloom of the weather and the chill facade of the castle itself. Then, abruptly, the woman I assumed to be our hostess released Denise from the affectionate hug and turned toward me with apology in her pale blue eyes. "Oh, and this lovely girl must be your nurse. How rude you must think we are, my dear Miss Reed! We have no telephone, and we were told there would be no flights from the mainland today because of the weather. It was only as a precaution I sent the car out. And here you are, thinking we are too careless to come and meet you."

Denise managed to squeeze in a casual introduction: "You know this is Terry Reed,

Auntie, but she doesn't know *you*. Terry, this is my Aunt Ilse – Mrs. Westlake."

I barely had time to acknowledge the introduction with a nod. A soft pink hand, sparkling with rings, clutched at mine. "Denise's *grateful* Aunt Ilse. Her father has written to tell us how important you have been to our niece's recovery, darling. We can only show our gratitude by trying to make your stay here enjoyable. You will rest. It has been an ordeal for both of you, but now you have me and you have the servants to help you care for –"

"I don't need care!" Denise protested. "I feel great."

Ilse Westlake's pink-complected face shriveled in a disapproving maternal scowl. "You are to rest and to recover, child. It was a *terrible* illness, was it not, Miss Reed? Well, then. I have canceled all my social engagements so that the house will be quiet and –"

"Auntie, I hate quiet houses."

Denise's objections were waved aside. "You young people!" Ilse said, her tone that of an exasperated grandmother. "Oh, but here we stand arguing when you must be exhausted. Come, I will show you to your rooms, and then Denise must get into her bed."

Denise shot me a plaintive glance. "Tell her

31

I'm not an invalid, Terry! I'm fine! I want to see Uncle Durward."

Ilse, one of her fleshy arms around Denise's waist and the other around mine, ushered us into a dimly lighted vestibule. Either Ilse Westlake's taste in decor was better than her taste in clothes (the flowing chiffon dress, besides being inappropriate for the damp weather, recalled pictures I had seen of English garden parties during the nineteen twenties) or else she had employed a decorator to make the best use of antiques that belonged to the castle. The masonry walls had been recently painted in a fresh off-white, providing an effective contrast with dark wood paneling and massive, carved ceiling beams. Mahogany-colored tiles, brightly waxed, were left exposed except for a scattering of thick floral-patterned rugs that were visible in the enormous room beyond the entry hall.

Like the woodwork, the furniture was dark, ornate, and ponderous, yet any antique collector would have thought herself in heaven viewing the exquisite workmanship and design of the refectory table in the vestibule, the soft patina of the silver candelabra that graced it, the elaborate gold filigree picture frames surrounding the oil portraits – a veritable gallery of somber, aristocratic faces that vied with priceless-looking tapestries for attention.

We had entered the large room, apparently one of a series of formal parlors, and I was wondering which of the rigidly posed, dark-eyed Spanish beauties who stared down at us from the walls had ended her days sealed in the masonry of this castle, when I realized that I had been so absorbed in my impressive surroundings that I hadn't been listening to the conversation.

"As you know," Ilse Westlake was saying, "your uncle has absolutely no social sense at all. If you think *this* is impolite behavior" – she released a tinkling, indulgent little laugh – "imagine my embarrassment when dear Durward refuses to make an appearance at one of my own dinner parties! However, I can't expect a scholar to be as devoted to correct social form as I am. We Gerhardts, after all, *lived* for our parties, our social functions. In those lovely days it would have been unthinkable for a host to excuse himself because he had to finish a chapter of his book."

"Is that what he's doing now?" Denise asked. She sounded more amused than annoyed.

Her aunt guided us toward a sweeping marble staircase that separated the enormous room we were in from another almost exactly like it. "Oh, yes. Try to be sympathetic, Denise. I have learned to forgive your Uncle Durward's little eccentricities. He practically lives in his library and that suffocatingly humid hothouse he had built next to it. But this is his life, and I try to adjust to it." Ilse turned the pink and blue roundness of her face toward me. "I do hope you don't think I am complaining, my dear. My husband believes that people should do exactly as they please, and consequently I *do* enjoy a pleasant social life, though I would prefer it if –"

"– the parties you give could be on as grand a scale as they were in Vienna," a male voice interrupted.

We were at the foot of the staircase, and along with Denise and her aunt, I turned to see an inordinately handsome man rising from one of the velvet upholstered couches. He had evidently been lying there reading, hidden from our view by the high back of the sofa. Now, a forefinger marking his place in the book he held, the man strolled casually in our direction.

Not much older or taller than I, his sparse frame was topped by a gleaming mass of wavy black hair. His eyes, too, were black, and rather closely set together in a slender face whose features resembled those seen in the portraits around us. With his neatly trimmed sideburns and slim moustache, his pale complexion and almost arrogant bearing, I decided he looked too much like a proud Castilian to be Durward Westlake – a guess that proved to be correct. Besides, from what I had heard of Denise's uncle, he wasn't apt to be wearing a wine-colored smoking jacket.

The stranger was smiling as he walked toward us – a flashingly bright but sardonic smile that crinkled the corners of his eyes, yet revealed more malice than good humor. When he spoke again, I noticed that his English was tinged with a pleasant Spanish accent.

"Unfortunately, none of us can recall our youth, Ilse. Nor can you hope to entertain as lavishly as you Gerhardts entertained before Hitler was inconsiderate enough to lose the war for you."

Ilse's already pink face flushed to a deep rose shade. "This is hardly an introduction to our other guests, Esteban." She looked from Denise to me with a flustered expression. "Señor Galvez is more gracious when he is not full of sherry." She made a curt introduction, adding to Esteban Galvez's name the fact that "Durward and I call him Steve."

"Among other names," Steve murmured. His look of amusement had centered on me.

"Ilse has told me that this will be your first visit here. If I were a native, I would feel obligated to apologize for the weather, Miss Reed. In spite of my love for *jerez* – for sherry – I *am* civilized enough to wish that you had been welcomed by Majorca's more typical sunshine."

"You don't live here, then?" I asked.

Steve Galvez shrugged his shoulders. "At the moment I am one of those houseguests who threaten to become a permanent fixture. However, my birthplace is Barcelona, I was educated in Paris, and my favorite city is Florence." He made a slight bow in Ilse's direction. "Currently, I assist Ilse in balancing the guest list when Durward refuses to be torn from his study."

"Steve and Durward became friends through their common interest in botany," Ilse explained. She was being polite, but it seemed to me that she was registering disapproval; letting it be known that Esteban Galvez had been brought into the household by her husband.

Apparently the Westlakes' "permanent fixture" caught that inference, too, for he repeated his courtly bowing gesture, with its subtle overtone of ridicule, and said, "Unfortunately, my humble knowledge does

36

not offer a great conversational challenge to an expert of Durward's caliber." Steve smiled directly at me, as though inviting me to share some private joke. "Senora Westlake has been attempting to arouse my interest in astronomy. *Que lástima!* What a pity I do not have an interest in old and fading stars."

Although the remark was addressed to me, it was obviously some sort of dig at our hostess. Ilse responded by turning her back on Steve and speaking to Denise and to me, as though no one else was present. "There is always an exception to prove every rule, is there not?" she said quietly. "Señor Galvez is determined to prove to us that the Spanish are a remarkably courteous people. We might forget that if it were not for an occasional *a*typical example to remind us." She glanced over her shoulder, acknowledging her handsome houseguest once more. "If you will excuse us, Steve, Miss Reed is anxious to get her patient to bed, I am sure."

Denise, who had been saying nothing at all, let out an exasperated whoop. "That's ridiculous! Dr. Addison didn't say anything about . . ." She looked to me for verification. "Do I have to be treated like a critical case, Terry?"

I assured Ilse Westlake that Denise was to avoid overexerting herself, but that, in general, her doctor had said that she could resume normal activities. "As a matter of fact," I said, "I'm beginning to think that her father sent me along because Dr. Addison said the case had exhausted *me*."

Denise laughed. "You see, Aunt Ilse? I'm going to tuck my nurse into bed and see if I can find someone to play tennis with."

Tennis was still out of the question for Denise, of course, and the weather would have precluded a game in any event. But Steve Galvez responded seriously to the facetious announcement. "What a pleasure it will be to have two such lovely competitors! Frankly, Ilse, I have given up trying to teach your aging protégée how to play. She uses the game as an excuse to pursue me." Steve rolled his dark eyes ceilingward. "Perhaps she would stop foisting her company on me if you made it clear that I have no intention of marrying *anyone*, and certainly not an unsuccessful actress who is desperately looking for a – what do the Americans call it? – a meal ticket."

Visibly angry now, Ilse started up the steps. "Come, girls. Steve is being viciously un-Spanish again."

Denise remained motionless, her eyes

38

narrowed in suspicion. "This ... actress. This other houseguest. That wouldn't be Anita Alma?"

Steve Galvez nodded solemnly. "It would be, and it is."

Ilse retraced her steps hurriedly. "I know you did not care much for Anita, but *do* try to understand, Denise. She's my dearest friend, and she has had so many terrible reverses in recent years."

"Maybe I'd *better* go to bed," Denise muttered between her teeth. "Suddenly I feel violently sick to my stomach."

"Ach, Denise!"

Ilse's consternation was pitiful. I found myself sympathizing with her loyalty to a less fortunate friend, and regretting Denise's selfish attitude. Like Steve Galvez, she was a guest in her aunt's home, and her manner was unthinkably rude.

"I often suffer from the same disability," Steve said lightly. He appeared to be enjoying Ilse's discomfort. "Yet, if one has a sense of humor, Anita can be amusing, no?"

Denise threw him a baleful glance. "She'd have to drop dead to amuse *me*."

The handsome Spaniard smiled his delight with the retort. "In my case, the desire for mayhem would be more complex," he said. "I would rather cut my throat than find myself married to Anita. And if I go on rejecting her in my usual barbarous fashion, there is an excellent possibility that Anita will perform that little chore *for* me."

"You must know," Ilse said, "that Señor Galvez will say anything outrageous to call attention to himself." She linked her arm through Denise's, urging her away from the scene. "You will learn to ignore his poisonous attempts at wit, dear. As for you, you are much too sweet a child to be serious about your attitude to poor Anita. I am sure you will become the best of friends."

Ilse Westlake's pacifying comments ended the awkward discussion; probably out of consideration for her aunt, Denise let the subject drop. Soon afterward, as we explored the adjoining second-story rooms, that had been assigned to us, Denise was once more the happy, enthusiastic teen-ager I had learned to love, excitedly pointing out the museum pieces with which our spacious, tile-floored quarters were furnished, making certain that I looked down from our ornately iron-barred windows to see the flower-filled patio below, and fully appreciated the moss-covered stone fountain that centered it. The rooms across the hall enjoyed a vista of the village and the bay, but Denise had written ahead, asking that her room overlook the brick-paved terrace with its quaint Old World benches and planters, and scrollwork gates at the ends leading to tiny hidden gardens. She was ecstatic about it now, and eager for my reaction. In other words, Denise was being Denise again, and her aunt, enormously pleased by the brighter atmosphere, was so busy competing for a chance to join the chatter that not only was Anita Alma forgotten, but nothing more was said about treating Denise like an invalid.

Apparently I was the only one who remained haunted by the implications of hostility that existed between Denise and Miss Alma. I was vaguely disturbed, too, by Steve Galvez, though, strangely, considering my dislike for people who made uncharitable personal remarks about others who were not present, I found myself attracted by his blunt honesty; certainly he did not mask his sentiments behind the flowery phrases so often associated with Latins. Instead of sounding vindictive he had struck me as a man removed from others, throwing out shocking statements and then standing back and studying the results with scientific detachment. Polished, educated . . . how else could anyone interpret his ungentlemanly statements?

41

FIVE

Although it is another dinner at the castle that is permanently seared into my memory, I have a clear recollection of the first time I sat down with the Westlakes and their guests at the banquet-sized table in the castle's baronial dining hall.

There were six of us present; besides Denise and myself, there were, of course, our hosts, Ilse and Durward Westlake, Steve Galvez, dapper in Continental dinner clothes, and, just returned from a cocktail party in the capital, Anita Alma.

In the Spanish fashion, the meal was served late; it was nearly ten o'clock by the time we were seated. Durward Westlake had been coaxed out of his lair by Ilse only moments earlier. A tall, bony, stoop-shouldered man in his mid-forties, he wore the abstracted air of a preoccupied scholar, his small gray eyes peering past everyone unseeingly through thick, steel-rimmed glasses. He had wispy blond hair that had gone uncut for a long time, and fell in straight strands from a carelessly combed center part. With his gaunt frame, sallow complexion, and weak

42

features (I particularly remember a receding chin that tapered to an abrupt point almost directly under his barely dilineated mouth), he bore no resemblance at all to his brother, except for the color of his eyes.

Denise's warm hug had been acknowledged by a vague smile and a nasal murmur: "Ah, yes. I heard you would be coming today." Durward had only nodded at me when Ilse introduced us, though it was impossible to be offended by this mild, other-worldly man. He was not unfriendly, I decided; he was simply uninterested in everything outside his field of study.

Anita Alma, on the contrary, was extremely interested in me, though I would have preferred not to be examined as though I were an adversary in some upcoming battle. In spite of Steve's disparaging remarks, Anita was still attractive; "aging" was hardly a description for a fortyish woman who had kept her svelte figure, and had been blessed with finely hewn, classic features, and an almost translucent ivory-toned skin.

At a casual glance, one would have called Anita beautiful. Ironically, her attempts to perpetuate that beauty were the very factors that marred it. Her hair had been hennaed to a glaring orange-rose shade that only served to emphasize the inevitable age lines around her face. Severe dieting had probably caused the unfirm flesh under her chin and the scrawny appearance of her neck and arms. She had sultry green eyes, but the soft color was overshadowed by a heavy application of mascara and eye shadow and her own assets would have glittered more without the competition of too much jewelry.

Still, in the black taffeta gown she had worn to the cocktail party in Palma, she was a striking figure. Why, I wondered, did she examine Denise and then me with such frantic, competitive appraisal? Why was every movement a self-conscious pose, every ripple of laughter a theatrical affectation?

This seemed to have an adverse effect on Steve Galvez; where I pitied Anita's misguided attempt to cling to her beauty, and to find a husband, he apparently derived a sadistic joy from needling her.

While we consumed our *Paella Valenciana,* a complicated dish that Ilse's cook had prepared for Denise's homecoming, Steve turned his wry gaze toward Anita. "You have not told us whether you had a successful trip this afternoon, Anita. Tell me, was the cocktail party worth the expenditure of all that new regalia? Did you meet any prospects . . . a retired stock broker, perhaps? A few stray colonels, suitably widowed?"

Anita made a stab at laughter, but she was plainly embarrassed. Her attempted gaiety fell somewhat flat. "You should have come with me, Esteban. I *did* invite you, darling."

"Yes, but I have seen these tiresome expatriate faces often enough," Steve said. He drained his wineglass and motioned to the serving girl for a refill. "By staying here, I knew that I would be treated to the sight of fresh, *young* faces." He paused while his wine was poured, then lifted the glass shakily; there was no doubt that he had already drunk too much. "A toast to La Alma and her conquest of Palma." He grinned at me impishly. "Do you know what *la alma* means in Spanish, Terecita? *Soul.* The soul. Is that not romantic? A pity the motion picture producers never saw beyond the body . . ."

Ilse cleared her throat meaningfully. Anita's smile had frozen on her face, but the heavily fringed green eyes darted venom at Steve. There was a painful silence, and then, surprisingly, Durward Westlake spoke; until then, he had been paying no attention to any of us. "Too bad I didn't know you were going to Palma. You could have checked on a shipment of books I've ordered." As though everyone else was superfluous, he confided to Steve, "I ordered the Albertus Magnus volume I've been wanting for years. Original

45

edition, old boy. 1786."

Steve nodded. "Yes, I know. A priceless volume, Durward. I daresay the same expenditure would have paid the cook her back wages for the past three months, and left enough to support you for the –"

"It has only been *two* months," Ilse muttered. It was her turn to blush and to glare at Steve. "And the servants are not complaining. Eventually, they always get their salaries."

I felt like an eavesdropper, hearing the discussion of what were obviously strained and garbled finances. Durward, however, did not share my discomfort. "Yes, with my brother increasing our allowance now that Denise is here, I shouldn't think we'll have to scrimp." He looked over his glasses at his niece. "Your father still driving himself at that insane pace?"

Denise nodded glumly. "It doesn't do any good to tell him to slow down."

Durward shrugged his long shoulders – bony in spite of the old-fashioned shoulder padding of his wrinkled tweed suit jacket. "One of these days Walter will push himself too hard, and then we won't have to economize at all. I'll buy original herbals instead of reprints, and Ilse will give a party every night."

46

Denise drew a sharp breath. "That's a *terrible* thing to say!"

Flustered, Ilse tried to cover up the blunt prediction. "Your uncle does not mean that, dear. He is so ... how do you say ... wrapped up in his work, he does not ..." She paused, unable to excuse the cold statement, and I recalled that as Durward had come out of his study he had been bemoaning the sickly condition of one of the plants in his hothouse, his compassion that of a parent with a sick child. Now, his calloused and unabashed reference to his brother's imminent death made it clear that Durward Westlake considered plants considerably more important than people.

There were other chilling statements at the table that night. I felt as though I were stationed in a crossfire of hostilities. There was Anita's question about Walter Westlake: "I meant to ask, Denise ... how *is* your charming father? I had hoped that he might be coming with you."

"I'll *bet* you did," was Denise's reply. It was followed by a tense silence, during which Ilse seemed unable to think of anything to say, and Steve Galvez smiled his cool amusement, as though these inter-personal frictions were a game in which he reveled.

I was relieved when the meal was finally

finished. Durward returned to his study. Ilse said something about having to make an appearance at a party being given by new American neighbors in the villa nearest to the castle. Steve and Anita, carrying the remaining supply of dinner wine with them, continued their barbed exchanges over a game of gin rummy in one of the mammoth sitting rooms. I was glad that Denise finally admitted that she was tired and wanted to get to sleep.

Sometime during the dinner, the rain had started to come down in earnest. Long after Denise had fallen asleep in her own room, I lay awake, listening to the heavy raindrops pelting my window, and letting a kaleidoscope of unrelated thoughts drift through my mind.

Although it was unlikely that Denise would need me during the night, (indeed, except to remind her to take her vitamins, she did not need me at all!) I had left a small lamp lighted on the night table beside my bed. Now, almost too weary to sleep, I reviewed the events since I had left New York.

It seemed hardly possible that I was in a castle overlooking the Mediterranean, surrounded by people like none I had ever known before. Was this the "wholesome family atmosphere" Walter Westlake had wanted for his daughter – relatives who lived off his bounty and ignored their

48

debts to pamper their extravagant tastes? A Continental playboy whose cruel wit was matched only by his capacity for liquor? Or an equally dissipated female whose life seemed dedicated to finding a rich husband?

Remembering snatches of the dinnertime conversation, I let my eyes wander over the room. Everything here was spacious and massive. There were fourteen bedrooms in the castle, Denise had told me, and apparently the Westlakes' funds had not covered the refurbishing of these seldom-used guest quarters. Although the room had been thoroughly cleaned, the yellow tile floor waxed and polished to a mirrorlike finish, a sense of decay hung over it, as though ancient dust and cobwebs had left their essence in spite of Rosalia's efforts with mop and broom. Had the lady with the cats ever occupied this canopied bed? I wondered. Had she walked across that now shabby, deep red rug with its intricate Moorish design in yellow-gold, or pulled aside those heavy amber velvet draperies to look down at the rain-spattered courtyard below?

Abruptly, my questions shifted to more practical matters. Even in this remote village area, a sumptuously furnished castle of these proportions must be costly to rent and maintain. Did Walter Westlake support two perfectly able adults because he was impressed with his brother's scientific pursuits, or was he merely a generous fool? Did he know that he was also providing room and board for a pair of semipermanent houseguests, who seemed content to live as leeches?

Random thoughts in an atmosphere of strangeness. Yet, though I had thought myself too overstimulated to sleep, my eyes were closed and I was becoming aware only of the hushed sound of rain when another sound imposed itself upon my consciousness. Someone . . . something was scratching at my door.

I sat up in bed, listening intently. The noise was repeated, this time accompanied by a distinct *meow*.

I should have been relieved to know there was nothing outside my door but a cat. Instead, my breath congealed inside my lungs, and my heart began an uncontrollable, audible tattoo.

How many seconds I sat there, motionless, seized by irrational fear, I do not know. Then, in a flash I realized the incongruity of my fright. I adored cats and kittens; as a child, having a kitten of my own had been a consuming desire. Now, just because I had heard a gruesome legend involving felines (a story probably colored in the retelling), I was behaving like a terrified idiot! Swinging my feet out of the bed, without stopping to slip into my robe, I padded across the small rug and over the contrastingly cold tiles to open the door.

I did not scream; I was too shocked to do anything but draw in a gasping breath. Kneeling before my threshold, reaching to pick up a scrawny half-grown black cat, was a man.

Under the circumstances, any stranger would have startled me. But the face that looked up into mine inspired pure horror. Set on a thick, squat body, with no neck at all visible, the enormous round head with its shaven dome resembled some grotesque vegetable rather than a human form. The flesh, covering coarse, distorted features, was a pallid yellow. The man's mouth was so grossly deformed that I could only think he had been born with a harelip and cleft palate, and that the attempt at reconstruction had been cruelly botched by an inexpert surgeon. Most shocking of all were the watery blue eyes, strangely familiar, that stared up at me in fright.

It may have been that expression, and the realization that this pathetic creature was more shocked by my sudden opening of the door than I had been by the sight of him, that kept me from dissolving in sheer hysteria. I managed to make some inane reference to the cat, and I forced myself to smile.

I was rewarded with a guttural grunt as the man got to his feet. (They were tiny feet, I noticed, encased in muddy hightop boots that had probably been fashioned for a ten-year-old boy.) In about the same instant I remembered where I had seen the anachronistic black serge jacket and trousers; this was the man I had seen, his back turned to me then, hoeing in the garden.

Queasy under a wide-eyed gaze that had not left my face, I said, "You're the gardener, aren't you? And is that your cat? Probably ran into the house to get out of the rain."

If the man understood me, he was unwilling or unable to respond. As I stood in the half-open doorway, he backed away from me for a distance of three or four feet. In that moment the compassion that had replaced my fear gave way once more to a shuddering revulsion. The man was carrying the struggling cat in a grip that only a retarded or sadistic mentality could have conceived. He had closed two short, sausagelike fingers around the animal's neck, letting it hang suspended in the air. With the other hand, paradoxically, he was petting the black fur with gentle strokes. And as the creature pawed at the air in a vain attempt to escape, I saw the two stubby fingers tighten and realized with shock that the rest of the man's hand was missing.

For a few horrifying moments he stood there, seeming to be as paralyzed as I was. Then, as I opened my mouth to suggest that he support the cat's weight with his free hand, the man whipped his body around – a stunted but powerful body that looked as though it had been compressed by heavy weights – and ran awkwardly down the long corridor to the stairway.

Long after I had locked my door and returned to my bed, shivering as though I were a malaria victim, the man's pathetic face and the crippled hand clutching the cat's neck burned themselves into my consciousness like sequences in an unforgettable nightmare.

Most disturbing of all was remembering that the man had been *petting* the cat, at the same time squeezing out its breath with a vicelike grip. He hadn't wanted to hurt it, I decided; behind his blank eyes there was a feeble, twisted mind; the man was clearly subnormal. Disturbing, too, was the familiarity of those eyes ... round, pale, bulging. They were the eyes of Ilse Gerhardt Westlake.

SIX

Although it was nearly daybreak before I fell asleep, I awoke refreshed, to a glorious morning of sunshine and birdsong. Denise, I discovered, had risen early, and over her aunt's protests had accepted an invitation to drive down to the village with someone named Van Stuart.

With no one else in sight (Durward had already confined himself in his study, and apparently the other houseguests didn't stir before noon) I found myself having breakfast in a pleasant sun-room with Ilse.

She was in a swivet about her niece's departure. "I did not want to disturb you, Terry," she said. "Yet my conscience burns that I did not. You might have convinced that stubborn child that she must not endanger her health. Imagine, going out with that young man, and she just escaped from her death bed!"

"Denise *was* seriously ill," I assured her aunt. "But there's no reason why she can't go out and enjoy herself now. She's quite a sensible girl." Ilse looked dubious, and I smiled at her overconcern. "Tell me about the young man. Is he someone Denise met last time she was here?"

"No, no. He is the son of the new occupants of the villa . . . look, you can see the spires above that clump of trees there. No – look down the mountainside and to the south. The Stuarts have leased the place, and their son is visiting them. People from California. Enough money, it appears. I spent an hour at their housewarming last night and . . ." Ilse sighed disconsolately. "I made the mistake of mentioning my niece to young Stuart. He was here this morning almost before I had opened my eyes. This is a ridiculous hour of the morning to be having breakfast. Nine thirty!"

I checked my watch. "I'm usually up several hours before this."

"Ach, well. This is good. You were tired from the long trip," Ilse said.

"Yes, and then last night . . ." I stopped, reluctant to tell my hostess about the incident with the gardener. The man had done no harm, and I certainly didn't want to jeopardize his job by revealing that he had frightened me.

"And last night?" Ilse repeated. "Something happened? You were ill? You did not sleep well?"

She was so solicitous that I finally told her what had kept me awake until nearly daylight, emphasizing that my fright had

55

been the result of fatigue and an overactive imagination.

Instead of being annoyed with a servant who had disturbed one of her guests, Ilse Westlake shook her head sadly. "Ach, Rudi. You must forgive him, Terry. He is not . . ." She tapped her forehead significantly. "You understand."

"He's retarded?"

"Yes. Yes. And it is more tragic yet. Rudi . . . you must promise not to tell the neighbors . . . I try so hard to protect the family . . . our reputation." Ilse's eyes had filled with tears and she blinked them back. "He has been in trouble with the law. Strange things . . . he was never able to understand what is right, what is wrong. But they will not keep him in a mental institution, and he cannot earn his living. What can I do? I live in fear, if I do not take care of him, he will . . . commit some crime. So I see that he has a home, and his pets – even as a little boy, he would like to keep a bird, a cat." A visible shudder ran through Ilse's body. "So often, a pet would die. He is so strong, Rudi. So strong; he does not know . . ."

"You said you try to protect the family reputation," I said. "Is Rudi a . . . ?"

"My brother," Ilse said. "You are a nurse. You know of such things. How can I send him

56

away? Here, he does no harm. He works in the garden. And he looks to me . . . I am all he has. Whatever I say, Rudi will do. He is almost forty years old, Rudi, but he is like a child. So, you see, it is safe for him to be here, where I can watch him."

I agreed, assuring Ilse that I sympathized with her problem and respected her compassion for the mentally ill. "Now that I understand . . ."

"You will be kind to him, yes?" Ilse's eagerness was touching. "I am so sorry for you to meet Rudi under bad circumstances. I . . . should have introduced you. But yesterday was . . . you know." Ilse made a flighty gesture with her plump hand. "Everything up in the air, no? And Rudi does not have dinner with us since we have guests." There was a painful pause. "My poor brother, he is not good to look upon. Not all people are so sympathetic as you." Ilse reached over to give my hand a grateful pat, and no more was said about Rudi Gerhardt.

My encounter with Rudi was forgotten, lost in the pleasant developments of that first day in Majorca. First there was Denise's irrepressible happiness as she introduced me to the young man who had appeared at her doorstep as if his presence had been planned especially for her benefit. Her delight was understandable; Van Stuart was one of those tanned, blond, muscular specimens that seem indigenous to California. Nor was brawn his only asset; he had a quick, engaging smile and a puckish, open expression to complement a pair of deep blue eyes that looked directly at the person he was addressing. There was nothing brash about his manner, and I decided almost instantly that he was someone who could be trusted.

"Isn't it a coincidence?" Denise asked as the three of us sat in the courtyard later that morning. "Van had an accident just like I did. And he was out of school so long, he messed up this semester and gets to goof off until next fall."

Van grinned, revealing teeth that would have done credit to a toothpaste manufacturer. "We've had a ball this morning, comparing operations."

"Silly!" Denise's admonition indicated a warm intimacy. "He's just jealous because I was *really* wracked up. All he had were a couple of measly fractures. Skiing. I got hurt ice-skating. That's a crazy coincidence, too, isn't it?"

"I've known life-long friendships that had less to go on," Van said, winking at me. "The thing is, with all Denise and I have in common, who gives the seal of approval if a guy wants to take her beachcombing? I was going to ask her aunt, but I have a hunch you'll be easier to get along with, Miss Reed."

"You're making me feel like an old Spanish *dueña*," I told him. "Look, it's fine with me, if you'll just remember to take it easy. You know. No surfing, or anything strenuous."

"I won't even let her pick up a heavy seashell," Van promised facetiously. "Okay, Denise. Let's split before your aunt gives us another lecture about your infirmities."

"She means well," Denise said. She hesitated. "I dunno about leaving you, Terry. I mean ... it's kind of crummy to ..." Torn between loyalty and the natural desire to be alone with her new admirer, she said, "Wouldn't you like to come with us?"

Her invitation emerged so plaintive, and so hopeful that I would decline, that Van joined my laughter. "As an actress you're a great ice-skater," he said. "Come on – Miss Reed's too young and pretty for the chaperone bit."

It was wonderful to see Denise tripping off on a date, especially when I remembered despairing for her life just a short time ago. Yet my happiness for her only served to intensify my own loneliness. This was a significant moment, for it explained my brief association with Steve Galvez.

That afternoon, when Steve offered to
59

acquaint me with the quaintness and charm of Majorca, I had a choice between sitting at home and brooding about my unrequited love for Craig Addison, or making the most of an experience that might not be repeated in my lifetime. My decision did not ease the pain of my longing for Craig, but it opened the doors to uncounted beautiful sights, and the sophisticated company of a man who could be an interesting companion in spite of his caustic tongue and often boorish manners.

During the next week, with Steve Galvez as my constant guide, I lived in a wonder world that included a trip to the Drach Caves at Porto Cristo, where haunting music accompanied our boatride around an underground lake. We took a motor launch to the island of Formentor, picnicking in a secluded cove and then stopping on the way back to enjoy the colorful Majorcan dancers in the scenic little hamlet of Selma. Because I could not get my fill of looking at the crystal clear blue waters of the Mediterranean, Steve arranged to show me Palma's picturesque skyline from a sloop, courtesy of wealthy friends he had introduced at the Tomás Yacht Club.

During those whirlwind seven days, I traveled by the narrow-gauge railway at Petra for a spectacular view of the island.

I played tennis at the club at Calvo Sotelo, visited the Valdemosa monastery where, Steve told me, Chopin and George Sand had once carried on their stormy romance, and the eighteenth-century home of Junipero Serra, founder of California's missions.

There were excursions to lovely beaches that lived up to their romantic names; Arenal, San Vicente, Camp de Mar. One day in which I was introduced to the thrill of skin-diving (to Steve's disappointment, and to my relief, we encountered none of the giant rays that were our intended quarry!), we managed also to tour Majorca's exciting little shops, where, from a dazzling array of sequin and pearl-embroidered hand-knits, I chose a beautiful white stole. I wore it that evening, adding glamour to a date that started with dinner, in a framed patio restaurant off the Plaza Gomila, the "gossip's square," in Palma. My first vol-au-vent with lobster, there, was followed by a tour of "firsts"; listening to flamenco artists in a cavelike night club, dancing to calypso and other West Indian rhythms in a spot that featured the music of Surinam, capped by a lecture from Steve on Spanish history, with the mammoth barrels of a wine cellar serving as our background.

That week seems unbelievable in retrospect, considering that I had come to Majorca as a nurse and not as a vacationing tourist. Yet it was perfectly logical then; Denise not only required no care, but would have actually resented any interference with the exhilarating good times she was enjoying with Van Stuart. As I had pointed out to her aunt, Denise was a sensible girl; in her anxiety to make up for her close brush with death, she would not be foolish enough to jeopardize her health. And any pangs of guilt I might have had about not earning my salary were brushed aside by Denise herself; over and over she assured me that her father had *wanted* me to think of the Majorca trip as a vacation. "It's the only way he could think of," Denise said, "to thank you for all you did for me."

Proof that I wasn't neglecting Denise shone in her eyes. "In spite of what my aunt says, that rosy color you see on my face isn't fever," she grinned. "It's sunburn and" – Denise released a mock sigh of ecstasy "the first flush of ta-rue l-ove." Her tone was facetious, but I sensed that Denise was burlesquing emotions that were genuine; she was falling in love. Seeing her with Van, noting how ideally suited they were for each other, I couldn't have been more pleased. But when she probed for information about my relationship with Steve, my scoffing dismissal of a budding romance was equally genuine. "He's been the perfect platonic buddy," I said. "I'd be happier if he drank less, but I can't say that he hasn't been a gentleman."

Denise appeared skeptical. "Really? You mean Anita doesn't have any reason to look daggers at you?"

"Does she?" I asked.

'*Does* she!" We had been exchanging post-date confidences in Denise's room, and now she flopped across her bed, unconcerned about wrinkling a forest green suit that had been one of her bon voyage gifts from Walter Westlake. " 'Course, she looks daggers at *me*, too, 'cause she thinks I goofed up her big romance with Daddy. But you're a real contender. I mean, with Steve she at least has *hope*."

I was puzzled. "I'll admit he's attractive, in a . . . kind of snide, sarcastic way. But you told me Anita's object was marrying *money*."

Denise blinked her gray eyes at me. "So?"

"So . . . I know he has rich friends. He's on chummy terms with all the international set . . . all those swank people with villas at Cala d' Or. And I know he's spent a ridiculous amount of money showing me around. But he can't possibly fulfill Anita's requirements. If he could, he wouldn't be living here, sponging off your uncle and aunt."

Denise shook her head. "You're hopeless,

Terry. Haven't you gotten the bit?" Out of sophistication that belied her years, and from lifelong observation of the rich and the would-be rich, she had developed a sense for separating the two categories. "Don't you see, Steve's *loaded*. At least he will be, when his aunt dies."

"His aunt?"

"He calls her Tía Victoria," Denise said. "I gather she's one of those super-proper Spanish aristocrats. Old maid, lives in Barcelona, and I guess he gets a fat allowance from her. Anyway, the whole shebang here owes him all kinds of money. I know he's made loans to Anita. Ilse and Durward can't support their hobbies on what my dad sends them. They're in to Steve for a pile of pesetas, too."

Steve's new image as a silent benefactor instead of a leech clarified Anita Alma's sullen attitude toward me. Yet I might have gone on accepting Steve's casual invitations, except for a shocking occurrence that returned me to my duties as a nurse. More than that, the unexpected calamity was the beginning of change in the lives of everyone residing at the castle – a change that introduced the terrors of death, and death itself.

SEVEN

It began when Ilse Westlake asked me into her husband's study one morning, telling me that we had "something vital to discuss."

Durward was present when we entered the book-lined room with its adjoining hothouse. Apparently he was to be included in the discussion, though slouched in a huge leather chair, his face appearing as wrinkled and unkempt as his tweeds, he gave every indication of boredom with the interruption.

Ilse, a flouncy oversized butterfly in yellow chiffon, came as directly to the point as her scattered mind permitted. "Terry, you have got to help us. But you must not, no, not for one moment, consider this as a criticism of your activities here. I am delighted to see you discovering the charms of this place we love so well. Yet, I am at my wits' end regarding my niece."

"Is something wrong?" I asked. "Denise has never been happier, I'm sure."

"A child can kill herself with happiness," Ilse said. "Please believe me – I am not implying that you neglect your duty. On the contrary, my dear. As I told you, I have

65

curtailed my social activity in order to devote time to the care of Denise."

We were repeating our conflicting opinions about Denise's recuperation, when Ilse broke in, "You must understand, Terry, that we feel a grave responsibility for our niece. We are not only concerned about her – there is her father to think of. Poor Walter has already had two heart attacks. If Denise should suffer any reverses, the effect upon her father . . ." Ilse closed her eyes for a moment. "We would not know how to tell him."

Inwardly, I was questioning myself. Had I been too lax? Had Denise been getting enough rest? "What is it you would like me to do?" I asked.

"This matter of the fiesta tomorrow night," Ilse said. "We have been arguing about it for an hour."

"There's nothing to argue about." Durward sighed. "The girl's excited about going, the boy – what's his name? Stuart? – the boy has promised that he'll get her back here at a reasonable hour."

"It's an annual affair," Ilse explained. "In honor of the village's patron saint. Ach, Terry, I know young girls! There will be dancing and fireworks, drinking . . . all kinds of excitement. I am certain Denise will not sit on the sidelines. She will exhaust herself, and

I am so worried. I feel responsible, yet how can I order her not to go?"

My arguments about Denise's good judgment and Van's sense of responsibility had been gone over too many times to give Ilse any reassurance; she was genuinely distraught, and I had resigned myself to the disagreeable task of asking Denise to forgo the colorful event, when Durward Westlake came up with a compromise.

Getting up out of his seat with an air of impatient irritation, he said, "It's very simple. Terry will go with the pair and see that the girl takes it easy. Now, can we stop wasting time on trivial matters? I have my thaumaturgical fungi chapter to complete."

Ilse accepted his suggestion as though Durward had come up with something profoundly original. "Of course! Yes, that will satisfy everyone. I would have suggested that Steve go, too, but he has an old engagement to escort Anita and me to a dinner party in Palma ... important people we would not care to disappoint. Will you mind terribly, my dear? It should be delightful; if you have never attended one of these quaint rustic affairs ..."

Van and Denise were both gracious about the arrangement, doing their best to assure me that I would be welcome. Nevertheless, the gaiety surrounding San Ysidro's plaza the next evening was tempered by my feeling that I was a fifth wheel, putting a crimp into the fun of two young people who had, until then, enjoyed each other's company without benefit of a chaperone.

Brightly decorated booths had been set up around the grassy square, their lanterns and paper streamers as colorful as the flowers lining the cobblestone walks. A wave of tempting aromas rose from these little stands, attracting peasant families dressed in bright holiday finery. From a wrought iron bandstand in the center of the plaza, a valiant village band competed with strolling guitarists and the songs of early arrivals who had already imbibed a fair share of *palo*, the favorite Majorcan beverage. Children raced through the crowd, pelting each other with confetti-filled eggshells. With exploding fronds of palm trees silhouetted against an early evening sky of soft salmon-pink, with the green mountains darkening at sunset to form a somber backdrop for the festivity of San Ysidro, and the breeze blowing fresh across the child-sized bay, I should have been deliriously happy. Instead, I could only think of Craig Addison; of how different my perspective would have been if I had been walking through this delightful scene with my hand in his, instead of trailing along with two young people enamored of each other and merely tolerant of my inhibiting presence.

Shortly after nine o'clock, Denise, Van, and I had stopped for a respite in a charming little outdoor café just off the plaza. I was having a difficult time concealing any outward show of my intense loneliness, and Denise was reluctantly suggesting that perhaps we had better start for home. "If you're tired" Denise said, "or if you think Aunt Ilse will raise Cain if you don't get me back by ten, I . . . I can always see the dancers some other time."

She had been looking forward to the Catalan saldana dancing exhibition that was scheduled for nine thirty, and I had no intention of disappointing her because I was in a miserable mood. "I wouldn't dream of missing the dancing myself," I assured her. "Of course we'll stay."

"We shall stay until the stars have lost their glow and the moon turns blue," someone said.

We turned toward the direction of that familiar male voice. Peering out at us from a clump of banana trees in the corner of the amber-lighted patio was Esteban Galvez. His smile was radiant, if somewhat tipsy.

"It's Steve!" Denise cried. "How wild! I

thought you were in Palma with my aunt and . . . *it!*"

Steve moved out of his miniature jungle setting and stepped into the light, bowing gallantly and still grinning. "They have had the misfortune to be deprived of my scintillating company," he slurred. "I left them as we drove through the village. And since then, I have been a parched and weary searcher . . . seeking, seeking for friendly faces and" – he signaled a passing waiter – "refreshment for my drought-stricken throat. What will you have? Wine, Of course. What is a fiesta without wine?"

We were finishing ices, and when we turned down his offer, Steve ordered a bottle of sherry for himself and sat down at our table.

"Was Anita furious?" Denise asked hopefully.

"Savage," Steve replied. "She assured me that some day she will put a stiletto between my shoulder blades."

In spite of his condition and his sadistic delight in having spoiled Anita's evening, Steve brightened my spirits. His dark, flashy Latin handsomeness was enhanced by elegantly tailored dinner clothes, and he appeared to be in exceptionally high spirits. For a few minutes he regaled us with the details of his unspeakable rudeness to Anita,

70

relishing the telling as much as Denise enjoyed hearing the story. Then, since they were no longer obligated to keep me company, Van and Denise made an escape like that of a pair of paroled convicts, scurrying off to their freedom and leaving me with the enigmatic Spaniard.

As he sipped his wine, Steve's tongue loosened progressively, so that I found myself an unwilling but, somehow, curious listener to his opinions about the occupants of Castillo de los Tres Gatos. "Ilse is pathetic, of course. She dreams of holding salons for impoverished artists, though the closest she has come to supporting a struggling talent is the singularly untalented Miss Alma. Oh, and her pitiable attempts to woo the social *crème de la crème* of the expatriate colony! She has made herself a laughingstock among the very people she wishes to impress. Touchingly absurd!"

I squirmed in my chair, uneasy at listening to gossip about a hostess who had been unfailingly kind to me.

"Durward is a caricature, as you have no doubt observed," Steve went on. "It is as though he copied his dress and mannerisms from some ritual code on the characteristics of a science professor. Still, I can forgive him his lack of imagination; Durward, at least, is an expert in his rather exotic field."

71

I tried to change the conversation to more positive channels. "You're interested in botany, too, aren't you?"

"I am interested," Steve said rather imperiously, "in *everything*. Durward, unfortunately, has an interest so highly specialized that my rapport with him is limited to our mutual knowledge of herbological and mycological applications in necromancy."

I couldn't help laughing at the imposing sentence, and Steve's precise pronunciation of each syllable. He was making a studied effort to avoid slurring his words.

Steve laughed, too, and in that moment I found him extremely likable. "Yes, we are quite a gallery, all of us. Rudi the most fascinating, by far. This morning I found him in the rose garden, weeping profusely over the corpse of a poor little nightingale. I would have wept, also, had it not been for the fact that I was certain he had just twisted the bird's neck the way one turns a corkscrew. A revolting monster, Rudi."

"Why do you stay?" I asked. "With so much contempt for everyone in the household, why?"

"Oh, but they fascinate me!" Steve exclaimed. "I am a scientific dilettante, Terry. Under what microscope could I observe such fantastic specimens? No, no, with so many delightful new elements being added to the scene, with so many dramatic possibilities looming up on the horizon. I loathe having to tear myself away."

I wanted to ask what he meant by "dramatic possibilities," but Steve's last statement aroused my interest. "Are you leaving?"

He sighed. "Only long enough to pay a dutiful visit to my Tía Victoria. Occasionally it is necessary to replenish the bank account, and then it is necessary to fly to Barcelona and enact my role as a model nephew. My aunt is, as you might say, extremely straitlaced. In order to subsist, I am sometimes forced to endure excruciating periods of decorum and sobriety, calculated to maintain my good standing with the dear old girl." Steve drained his wineglass. "At times I wonder if it could be less effort to desert the ranks of the unemployed."

"You must suffer terribly!"

Steve accepted my wry comment in all seriousness. "I do. I detest lying, and I am forced to lie to stay in the good graces of my affluent relative." He laughed shortly. "For example, as far as Tía Victoria is concerned, I am currently studying at the Sorbonne. She would be hysterical if she learned that I am less than an hour away from Barcelona, enjoying my life."

As Steve continued his drinking and his increasingly personal revelations, my uneasiness mounted. Several times I suggested joining Van and Denise, only to have my companion urge me to stay. An hour or more had gone by before he said, "You are obviously unneeded as a nurse, and we have had such enjoyable times together. Why not come with me to Barcelona?"

I was aghast. "You can't be serious."

"Of course I am serious. The results would provide you with enough money to be able to go on vacationing for months, perhaps years. You see, my dear old spinster aunt has been obsessed with getting me married. If I introduced her to a lovely bride, her pocketbook would open to a magnanimous width. Why not?"

I rose to my feet. "If that's a proposal, I find it thoroughly insulting."

Steve managed to get out of his chair. "It was not, I assure you, a proposal."

Everyone else had deserted the patio when music for the saldana sounded in the plaza. Except for the waiter, who had disappeared inside the cafe, we were alone.

"It was not a proposal," Steve repeated. He smiled as his arms reached out for me. "It was the presentation of an opportunity."

74

Before I could move, I was swept into a powerful embrace. As I struggled to free myself, Steve's lips pressed against mine in a lingering, wine-sodden kiss.

Steve released me abruptly. He was smiling again, amused by my speechless fury. "How trite it is to say that you are beautiful when you are angry," he said softly. "Yet how true it is, *Terecita miá. Que lástima!* Victoria would have adored you."

I turned, brushing past him as I ran out of the patio. He made no attempt to follow me, and I ran toward the periphery of the throng gathered around the area marked off for the dancers. Tears of bitter rage blinded my eyes; I would have to get myself under control before I rejoined Denise and her escort.

I had slowed down and was walking along the edge of the crowd when I became aware of another circle of people. They were gathered around some other attraction, ignoring the entertainment and apparently excited about something. As I drew closer, a familiar voice stabbed at me:

"Stand back! Go get a doctor! Please ... somebody get a doctor. *Un doctor, por favor!*"

My heart stopped. It was Van, desperate in his attempt to communicate. I stood frozen for only a few seconds, then started pushing

75

my way through the gaping bystanders to where Van knelt, holding Denise's prostrate form in his arms.

She was lying still, her eyes closed and her face white with the deathly pallor I had seen so often during critical periods at the hospital. As I bent over her, Van's voice broke with mingled relief and agony. "Terry! We were just standing here and suddenly she collapsed! You've got to do something!" He was panicky; in his eyes was a fear that reflected my own.

I had barely begun to determine what kind of first aid was in order when a short, fleshy man in a threadbare black suit appeared at my side. He had a ring of fluffy white hair around his bald, leathery dome, and his deeply creased face wore a somber, scowling expression. From the way the people had moved aside to allow him to pass, I guessed that he was the local doctor.

I was right. Furthermore, he introduced himself crisply in heavily accented but understandable English. "I am Dr. Francisco Rivera." I made way for his ponderous body, giving him a breathless history of Denise's recent illness while he made his examination.

There was a nightmare period during which my guilt was almost as excruciating as my concern for Denise. I *hadn't* watched over her the way a nurse should care for a patient who has just been snatched from death's door. Yet she had appeared so vibrant and well; Craig Addision had given her a clean bill of health!

As I knelt to offer my assistance, telling Dr. Rivera that I was Denise's nurse, a pair of young men appeared with an improvised stretcher. "We take her to my office," the doctor ordered. "There." He indicated a small tile-roofed house facing the plaza. ⁻

There was no hospital in the tiny village, and I had to trust his judgment that Denise's immediate care ruled out a trip to the hospital in Palma.

It was within hearing distance of the gaiety of the fiesta that Dr. Rivera reached his diagnosis. Denise had regained consciousness by then, but the heavy-jowled old doctor insisted that she be allowed to rest undisturbed. In the shabbily furnished cubicle that apparently doubled as his reception room and living quarters, he faced me sternly. "If you are nurse to this patient, why she was permit to be in so great excitement?"

My attempt to explain was stopped by a wave of the doctor's hand. The nostrils of his small, beak-shaped nose were quivering with annoyance. "The young lady has the extreme irregular heartbeat and pulse. If you are so good a nurse" – his eyes blazed the opinion that I was *not* – "then why is not your patient in bed, with care of cardiologist?"

I could say nothing in my defense. During the next hour, Dr. Rivera checked and rechecked Denise's heartbeat, pulse, and temperature. Finally, appearing somewhat puzzled, he said, "There is not need to go to hospital now." Denise was fully conscious, murmuring that she felt only "kind of mixed up." We were given the doctor's approval to take Denise to the castle, with instructions that she be kept calm and that she was not to leave her bed. He promised that he would come to see the patient early the next morning.

It was a silent and fearful ride home. Van whispered, "Will she be all right, Terry? It's my fault. If anything happens to Denny, I . . . I don't know what I'll do."

The reactions at Castillo de los Tres Gatos were varied. Durward showed no interest at all, beyond an emotionless, "Well. That's too bad, isn't it?" Ilse, when she returned home from the dinner party after midnight, burst into tears and castigated herself for her "carelessness." Anita Alma said nothing, but there was a bemused expression on her face that chilled me. Even more upsetting was her comment that "this will be a terrible blow to Walter"; I would have sworn that she was relishing the idea that grim news might devastate the man who had rejected her.

There was an equally disturbing reaction from Steve Galvez. Late that night, when I had closed the door to Denise's room, assured that her pulse and temperature were normal and that she was peacefully asleep, I started down the hallway, intending to go to my room for a few minutes. Steve was standing in the corridor. He showed no sign of embarrassment over our last encounter. "How is she?" he asked.

I told him as much as I knew, including Dr. Rivera's sketchy diagnosis.

"Was there fever?" Steve asked. "Gastric disturbance?"

I told him there had not been, puzzled by his questions.

"Then perhaps I am wrong," he muttered, more to himself than to me. More directly, he said, "I would, if I were you, prepare all of Denise's meals myself. This may impose a burden upon you, Terry. However, until you decide to leave this place – and I am certain that you will – you will be wise to draw even the water Denise drinks directly from the tap."

His surreptitious manner and his hushed tone worried me, but when I asked for an explanation, Steve said an abrupt goodnight and retired to his room.

I spent a sleepless night trying to analyze those veiled remarks; was Steve seriously implying that someone in the castle might attempt to poison Denise? It was insane; she had suffered a cardiac irregularity, probably related to the damage that had been done during her bout with a staph infection. If Steve had reason to believe that Denise's life was in danger, why had he been so evasive when I asked my question? *Insane, inconceivable, absurd!* Yet in the dismal aura of the castle, in the dimly lighted room where I stood watch over my patient, it was easy to conjure up the most bizarre possibilities. I remembered that these walls had witnessed a grisly murder. Suddenly the very atmosphere was redolent of violence and evil. Somewhere in the garden, a cat released one of the diabolical yowls that I would have ordinarily dismissed as humorously typical of the feline mating season; now I shivered, and cold perspiration covered my forehead.

And at daybreak, while Denise still slept, I emerged from the room to find another of the castle's occupants outside the door. Rudi was there, a strange apparition in his ill-fitting

80

clothes, his hideous face turned toward me with a look of childish rapture.

He had never spoken to me before. Now, in broken English, and in a plaintive tone that sounded like wind sighing across a moor, he asked, "She be dead? She be dead, same as little bird?" Rudi's misshapen hand caressed the air, as though he were stroking some animate object. Then, as I made an effort to control my revulsion and told him that Denise was *quite* alive and resting comfortably, the hand from which three fingers had been amputated changed its unconscious action. Rudi was no longer petting an imaginary kitten. His sleeve had been pushed up, and I saw the powerful muscles of his forearm flex, forcing his thumb and one remaining finger into a crushing gesture. The bulging blue eyes shone with a maniacal light as the motion was repeated; the same motion he would have used to break the neck of a bird.

"She not dead," he wheezed. "She move? She not cold?"

My eyes remained fixed upon Rudi's disfigured hand.

81

EIGHT

Morning brought Dr. Rivera and an optimistic report; Denise's heartbeat and pulse had returned to normal. The old doctor shuffled out of the castle repeating his instructions to keep Denise in bed; any exertion might bring on another attack. Yet he admitted that the condition puzzled him.

"A simple village doctor," Ilse said when he had gone. "We cannot expect too much of him. But at least he is sensible, yes?"

I nodded miserably. Ilse had not openly reproached me for ignoring her earlier advice; was this a subtle reminder that I had neglected my duty? I made every effort to keep Denise calm; not an easy task, since she insisted that she felt fine, that the doctor had found nothing wrong with her this morning, and that she wanted to see Van. The latter, sleepless with concern, had virtually set up camp on the Westlakes' doorstep, but because I had been wrong once before, I bowed now to Ilse's advice that a visit from Van would be "too stimulating" for Denise. "I am so afraid Walter will think we have not taken care of the child," Ilse said.

82

I told her that there was no need to disturb Walter Westlake with news of a relapse from which Denise seemed to be making a quick recovery. Nevertheless, I felt her doctor should be advised. That afternoon, my fingers trembling for more personal reasons, I wrote a letter to Craig Addison, telling him about Denise's collapse and of Dr. Rivera's discoveries. I made no mention of Steve Galvez's hints that perhaps the temporary heart condition had been deliberately induced; the thought itself had paranoiac overtones, and I didn't want Craig to think that his patient had been turned over to a hysterical ninny.

Everyone, even Durward, was gathered in the main living room when I came downstairs with my letter. "Where can I leave this to be mailed?" I asked of no one in particular.

"I will be going down to the village this evening," Steve offered. "I can drop it off for you."

Ilse interrupted her card game with Alma to say, "Durward is going to Palma in the morning. Put it on the refectory table with my mail, Terry. It will go out faster from the city."

It was a logical suggestion. I added my letter to the stack of outgoing mail on the vestibule table and thought no more about it. For how was I to anticipate the shocking discovery I made the next morning, when I walked down to the garden to give Van Stuart a report on Denise and a note from her? I had good news for Van. Denise was in excellent spirits and looked well; perhaps I would be able to persuade her aunt that a chat with Van would, instead of jeopardizing Denise's health, bolster her morale.

Van's pleased grin was accompanied by his handing me a lavishly gift-wrapped box into which air holes had been poked. "Thanks, Terry. Give her this to keep her company until she gets out of the isolation ward. Hold it this side up."

I accepted the gift for Denise, my curiosity aroused. "It's something *alive*, isn't it?"

Van nodded. "Right. Actually, it's from my mom. She raises Siamese cats. This is the pick of a new litter."

"It's a kitten?" I recalled my own youthful desires for a surprise like this. "Won't Denise be thrilled? Thank your mother, for her, please."

"Tell Denny its name is V.L.Y.," Van said. He waved, and started walking toward the driveway, where he had parked his sports car. "Crazy name for a cat, but she'll know what it means."

Anyone looking at the boy would have

84

known that the letters meant "Van Loves You," but I made a discreet pretense of ignorance.

Carrying the box gingerly, I started back toward one of the rear doors of the castle. Nearby, behind a clump of oleanders, I saw Rudi watching me with interest. Smoke curled up from an incinerator which had been screened by the planting of pink-flowering shrubs; Rudi was burning trash, one of his morning chores.

My first instinct was to do what everyone else did, when possible – to avoid contact with Rudi Gerhardt's ugliness. It had probably always been so, and no doubt he knew this. The emotional scars of knowing that were unimaginable. I decided it was cruel to punish him with a lack of friendliness just because his appearance disturbed me; I walked toward Ilse's unfortunate brother, greeting him with a warm, "Good morning, Rudi. Hard at work already, as usual."

Rudi's watery eyes had fixed themselves on the box containing the kitten, but he said nothing.

Uncomfortable, but determined to win Rudi's friendship, I told him that Denise was feeling better this morning; that I *knew* he would be happy to hear that, and that I was carrying a gift to the girl. "She'd be very happy," I said, "if you'd pick a few flowers for her, Rudi, I know she'd like that."

Had all faith in human love and kindness been ground out of this pathetic creature? Had his disfigured face and hand, his squat, malformed body made him the object of derision for so many years that no one could penetrate beyond that wall of pain and mistrust? "No flower," he hissed. "No from Rudi. No flower!" He appeared angry, turning around abruptly as though he were letting me know that I had interrupted his work and he had no more time to waste.

It was while I was standing there, wondering how to assure him that I was his friend, that I saw the familiar scrap of paper. It had fallen from one of the wastebaskets Rudi was emptying, dumping the contents into the pyre he had ignited in the brick incinerator. I bent down to pick up the crumpled paper, recognizing it instantly as a corner of the letter I had written to Craig Addison!

Why had it been destroyed? Equally disturbing; who had destroyed it? Someone who didn't want Denise to have proper medical care? Someone who would have gotten a morbid thrill if Denise had succumbed after that attack at the fiesta?

Indignation overcame my fear of

aggravating Rudi. "Where did you get this?" I demanded.

Rudi turned, glanced at the evidence in my hand, and displayed no reaction at all. Perhaps he had no knowledge of the letter. I was too distressed, and I stood on too shaky ground, to make an accusation. I pocketed the scrap and returned to Denise's room.

Watching Denise's delight with the contents of the package (an adorable Siamese kitten that had cuddled against her in the bed and had promptly fallen asleep) and seeing her eyes light up with joy when I delivered Van Stuart's message, it seemed inconceivable that anyone could wish to interfere with that happiness. There had to be some plausible and innocent explanation for the fact that my letter had been destroyed.

It was impossible to get that explanation from Durward Westlake. When I asked him about the letter that evening, he looked at me blankly and shrugged. "I mailed whatever there was to mail," he said. I sensed that he was irritated with having to give thought to such a trivial matter.

Ilse, on the contrary, was extremely upset by the matter. "Durward is so absent-minded," she said. "He may have dropped your letter and not noticed. Then, Rudi . . . he is told to burn papers he finds lying around on the grounds. One scrap is like another to him. Ach, Terry, I am so embarrassed . . . I am so sorry! You must write again, of course."

I didn't write another letter. First, there was my foreboding instinct that a second letter might suffer the same fate as my first. Second, Steve Galvez again spoke to me, this time with a subtle suggestion that "matters are not always what they seem to be." I was inclined to dismiss the latter "warning." I had begun to regard Steve as an odd character who enjoyed stirring up suspicions and then sitting back like a detached demigod to observe the reactions of lesser beings.

Steve could be ignored, but my own intuition could not. When I spoke to Van again that evening, I asked him to cable Craig Addison, telling him that I was concerned about Denise's heart condition and that he should communicate with me via the Stuarts.

It didn't occur to me at the time that this brief message, with its request for a surreptitious reply, would alarm the doctor. But less than twelve hours later, Van brought me a cabled response from Craig:

ARRANGING FOR COLLEAGUE TAKE OVER PRACTICE. EXPECT ME MAJORCA NEXT WEEK. REGARDS.

I had forgotten that Craig was more than Denise's physician; he was also a close family friend, and something of my fear must have come through to evoke that drastic decision.

Yet why did that fear persist? When I let it be known that Dr. Addison was coming to Majorca (a naive act that I later regretted) Ilse, for one, was enormously relieved. "Such a big responsibility, the care of a stubborn child who is ill! And when one has so little faith in old Rivera! It will be a blessing to have Dr. Addison here."

Durward showed his customary lack of interest, but Steve could not resist one of his snide digs; "Yes, you cannot risk losing the girl, can you, dear people? Inasmuch as her presence doubles your income from her father."

Ilse refused to dignify the remark with an answer, but Anita Alma was quick to come to her defense. "How rotten your mind is, Esteban! Since the girl is here, poor Ilse has been maintaining the atmosphere of a hospital. No small sacrifice, I am certain." Anita's presence, too, had interfered with the usual gaiety of the castle.

I had no desire to become involved in the petty bickering. During the next few days I avoided the others as much as possible, spending most of my time in Denise's room and doing my best to keep her pacified.

"*Why* do I have to stay in this stupid bed?" she argued.

I would have agreed with her, except for a second attack, during which her heartbeat slowed, accelerated rapidly, and then slowed again in a mysterious fashion that puzzled Dr. Rivera as much as it puzzled me. Her quick recovery was equally confusing. It was no time to talk of resuming normal activity. I began to pray for Craig's immediate arrival.

Then, while I waited for Craig, another bewildering development convinced me that my intuitive fears were not unfounded. Like the tragedy that still haunted the castle, this event involved a cat.

NINE

Denise's Siamese kitten must have run out when I carried the dinner trays in that evening. In any event, it was shortly before ten o'clock at night when we discovered that the kitten was not in the room, and when my search of the hallway proved futile, Denise was nearly in tears.

I knew that the kitten was more than just

a pet to Denise; it was a symbol of the budding affection that existed between Van and herself. Since the slightest emotional upset might have serious repercussions in a patient with a cardiac problem, I assured Denise that her Siamese probably hadn't wandered far away and I set out in search.

Steve Galvez, I remembered, had been talked into escorting Ilse and Anita to another of the dinner parties that separated the expatriate set from boredom. Durward had been urged to accompany them, and I presumed that he had gone.

At that hour, the cook and the two maids were asleep in an isolated wing of the castle, and as I crept down the stairs, I was unnerved not only by the oppressing silence, but by the realization that on the main floor I might be virtually alone with Rudi Gerhardt.

Breath suspended, I tiptoed from room to room, searching behind old scrollwork furniture, sometimes groping around in semidarkness because I didn't want to call attention to my presence by turning on a light.

To my apprehension was added the worry that if I stayed away any longer, Denise might decide to come downstairs to help me with the search. Yet I had gone through almost every room on the lower story without success, and I dreaded the thought of returning to Denise's room without the kitten in my arms.

I would not have gone into Durward Westlake's study if the door had not been slightly ajar. The kitten could easily have slipped through that opening, I decided; it was my last hope, and I pushed the door open all the way and stepped into my host's sanctum sanctorum.

There were dozens of places in that dimly lighted room where a kitten might hide. It might have fallen asleep on one of the lower bookshelves – even behind the books themselves. Beyond the study, the bright light illuminated the hothouse; its beams filtered in eerie patterns through masses of strangely shaped tropical plants.

I was peering behind a row of worn, leather-bound books when the sound of footsteps startled me. I spun around, fully expecting to see Rudi's grotesque face. Instead, silhouetted against the green-tinged light of the hothouse, I saw Durward Westlake.

I started to stammer out an explanation: "I'm sorry. I thought . . ."

"You thought I wasn't here," Durward cried. "Is that what you thought? That gave you the right to come snooping in my private quarters?"

I had never before heard Durward raise his voice above a weary mumble. Now, livid with rage, he was shouting at me in angry tones that reverberated from the walls.

I was almost speechless with shock. "I only came to look for . . ."

"I don't want anyone looking for *anything* in here!" Durward yelled. "Don't ever come into this room again! Understood? Now, *get out!*"

The fierce quality of that command terrified me. I knew it would be hopeless to try to reason with the man, and his fury had made my search for the kitten secondary; my only thought was to escape from that avalanche of hostility. My legs trembling under me, I raced out of the room. I had left the door open, but Durward must have crossed the room, because I heard the door slam shut behind me. The slam was like a gun shot, but at least I knew that I was free of the infuriated demon I had aroused.

Still shaking, I started for the staircase. I was wondering what I would say to Denise, when I heard the muffled sound of someone sobbing. I stopped, touched by the anguished sobs, knowing almost immediately that the person in distress was Rudi.

As I stood in the darkened parlor, surrounded by stern-faced portraits of people, long dead, who had once inhabited these gloomy premises, I heard another sound that

I identified, after an interminable, breathless period, as that of someone shoveling earth in the rose garden beyond the back terrace.

Once again, curiosity overcame my fear. Carefully staying within the shadows of the room, I crossed over to the French doors that opened onto the rear terrace.

A full moon bathed the garden in silver light, throwing macabre tree shadows across the fountain. Through the glass-paneled door, approximately twenty feet from where I stood, I saw Rudi. He had a garden spade in his hands, and his freakish body shook with the agonized weeping that had arrested my attention. For a few minutes I watched him as he strained to dig a hole next to one of the rose bushes. Then, laying the spade aside, he bent down to the ground. Under the flood of moonlight that illuminated the scene, I caught a flickering glimpse of his mutilated hand. Grasped between the lone finger and thumb was the limp shape of a small cat. Horror swept over me as I recognized Denise's beloved pet.

It was not merely the horror of knowing that Rudi had killed the kitten; it was more. This was a nameless dread that held me transfixed while the pitiful, furry little body was gently placed into its freshly dug grave, and while Rudi resumed his laborious shoveling efforts to cover it with the damp earth. This had been a mindless, senseless, deeply regretted killing of a creature Rudi must have loved. For, as the final spadeful of earth was thrown down, Ilse's demented brother dropped to his knees on the mound, his body wracked by almost inhuman cries of sorrow.

How long I stood there shuddering I don't know. It seemed a long time before I retraced my steps to the stairway, mentally rehearsing the story I would tell Denise; I had seen the kitten running toward the Stuarts' villa; tomorrow I would get Van to return it. The lie would pacify Denise, and time would ease her loss. I would not, *could* not tell her what I had seen in the garden. I dared not tell her why I would spend another sleepless, fearful night.

TEN

After my experience with Durward Westlake, and after the gruesome scene I had observed in the garden, I wanted nothing more than to leave the Castillo de los Tres Gatos and never return. Apart from these two experiences, I found the other residents irritating; Steve, with his hints of intended foul play, Anita Alma with her cold superiority, and even Ilse, whose overprotective attitude and martyrdom regarding her curtailed social life added to my discomfort.

Yet it would have been impossible, without terrifying Denise, to suggest that we leave. To begin with, she was a minor, and she had come to the castle because it was her father's wish that she do so. I could hardly whisk her away because of a few upsetting incidents, or because I didn't care for her eccentric relatives and their friends. Nor was I going to leave her here alone. Most important was her desire to be near Van Stuart; Denise would not have considered a separation just as their interest in each other was beginning to flower. Finally, for the sake of her health, it made no sense to leave at a time when Denise's personal physician was probably making frantic arrangements to turn over his practice to another doctor so that he could come to her aid. The fact that I was anxious to see Craig Addison myself also held me to my post. It was a time of uneasy waiting.

Somehow, the waiting was made easier the next day. Steve Galvez had announced his intention of leaving for Barcelona on the following morning, and somehow his projected departure (although he only planned to be gone for a few weeks) kindled a warm spirit of conviviality among the castle's residents. Ilse began relieving the tense atmosphere that had permeated the household by suggesting that perhaps a brief visit from Van Stuart might not be harmful to Denise. "The child is liable to do herself more harm by brooding," she said. "You *will* tell the boy to keep his visit brief, yes? And very quiet?"

I didn't bother to remind Ilse that I was an R.N., and that my judgment in the care of my patient might be better than hers. I had apparently made a terrible mistake in allowing Denise too much freedom; now I was expected to let her aunt take over responsibility. I hurried off to give Denise the good news.

While Van and Denise chatted in her room that afternoon, the rest of us sipped Madeira on the rear terrace. It was one of the warm, lazy, golden days for which Majorca is justly famous, and the conversation was as tranquil as the buzzing of bees in the garden surrounding us.

Durward Westlake, having exploded over the invasion of his private domain, apparently forgot the matter completely. Although he didn't apologize for his behavior, he held no grudge, either; I was accorded his usual casual indifference.

Anita, stretched out in one of her alluring poses, relaxed in a patio lounge with her eyes closed. Obviously bored with the conversation, which Steve and Durward seemed to be monopolizing, Ilse fidgeted, making desultory attempts to change the subject of discussion. Not unexpectedly, the talk centred around flowers.

"What an excellent place you have chosen for your studies." Steve addressed our host. "I sometimes wonder why you need the hothouse, Durward. Look around you. Aren't these common garden flowers the ones most closely associated with European witchcraft and folklore?" He indicated a stand of green spikes covered with purple and white blossoms. "There are peasants today who still believe that fairies and elves hide in those bell-like flowers. And how many other names the foxglove enjoys – most of them associated with the supernatural – goblin's cap, witch's thimble. An ethno-botanist whose prime concern is with the *use* of plants in sorcery, real or imagined, need only look into his garden. Consider the charming aconite buttercup. Call it monkshood or wolfbane, if you prefer."

Durward nodded impatiently. "Of course, of course. Any beginning student of the subject knows that the genus *Aconitum*

98

created numbing and flying sensations in medieval witches. These hallucinations no doubt account for the occasional confessions that were *not* extracted by torture. The poor demented creatures actually *believed* they had flown through the air. Obviously they knew enough to chew the leaves in small doses, otherwise the aconite would have paralyzed their nerves and muscles."

Steve turned his head, so that his smile took in all of us. "Aconite is a deadly poison, ladies. Only a witch may consume it with impunity."

Anita laughed without opening her eyes. "I adore it sprinkled over my breakfast cereal. Does that satisfy you, Esteban?"

Durward scowled at their light repartee. With dogged seriousness he went on: "Mythology has it that wolfbane sprang up first at the entrance to Hades. I have found references to the plant's properties in a treatise written in 1335 by Guy de Vigevani. And Hieronymous Mercurialis stated as long ago as the sixteenth century that our pretty little blue flower contains as antidote for scorpion bite, a fact obviously known by witches who claimed healing powers."

"Springwort, hawthorne, rue, fern, seed, the rose, betony, mugwort . . ." Steve had leaned back in his lawn chair and was droning

99

the names like a litany.

"But why do you persist in talking about the more obvious plants?" Durward demanded irritably. "What are we, Steve . . . wide-eyed neophytes in the field?"

"You are, if you will excuse me, darlings, a pair of pedantic bores." Ilse waved her lacy handkerchief as if she were brushing away a subject she found dull. "Can we talk about something of interest to *all* of us?"

"I was leading to that," Steve said with exaggerated graciousness. "Certainly we are all interested in the new guest you are expecting, Ilse." He turned to me abruptly. "Tell us, Terecita, does Dr. Addison have an interest in botany?"

I had to confess that I didn't know, adding, "I doubt that he has time for many interests outside medicine."

"Ah, but the subjects are inseparable," Steve argued. "He should be fascinated with some of Durward's rare old herbals. That priceless London Pharmacopoeia of 1650 you have just acquired, Durward. And the pamphlet published by a Dr. Withering in 1785 . . . what is the title?"

Durward tapped his pipe on the tiles of the terrace. "*An Account of the Foxglove and Some of Its Medicinal Uses.* Purely of historic value, Steve. A modern physician could hardly expect to learn anything new from its pages."

Strangely, a disquieting atmosphere had settled over our small gathering. Was it only because Ilse and Anita were uninterested in the topic, or was it because Steve's persistence in sticking to the subject indicated some barbed, as yet unfathomed, innuendoes? I only sensed that the air hung heavy with a deliberately created tension; what had caused it I could not begin to guess.

Steve's attention remained focused on me. "Yes, I am most anxious to return from my little trip and meet Dr. Addison. I am certain we will have much to talk about."

"Ridiculous," Ilse said. "A physician capable of curing Denise when dozens of specialists had failed . . . can you imagine such a man having time to discuss your exotic hobby? Dr. Rivera, perhaps, but not an American . . ."

"Quite the contrary," Steve insisted. "Medicine here in the Old Country sprang from folklore and necromancy. Our European doctors are so anxious to disassociate themselves from the superstitions that once plagued their profession that they tend to ignore even valid folk beliefs. I expect that an American doctor might be less inhibited." Steve's Machiavellian smile

101

encompassed the entire company once more. "And perhaps . . . more *curious*."

Ilse got to her feet. "You may be right. But, at the moment, I am ravishingly hungry and I would gladly exchange all your erudition for an early dinner." She looked around at the rest of us brightly. "What about the rest of you? We had such a miserable excuse for a luncheon."

"Not a phenomenal occurrence," Durward said. "Isn't that the customary procedure when the cook quits?"

Ilse blushed at the blunt revelation, but she made a brave stab at nonchalance. "We have survived worse catastrophes than the loss of Carmen. Shall we all pool our culinary talents? Invade the kitchen and pretend we are serfs?" Her laughter had the tinny, artificial sound I had learned to associate with Anita. "Wouldn't that be a quaint idea for a bon voyage party, darlings?"

"Quaint, perhaps," Durward said. "But the results would be revolting." He pulled his gawky frame out of his chair. "Suppose I volunteer my services?"

Anita applauded. "Bravo! You have so many talents, Durward, that I sometimes forget your genius as a gourmet cook."

"Something simple," Ilse suggested. "Omelets, perhaps – with some of your ingenious touches, love." Her forced gaiety told me that omelets were in order because eggs were probably all that would be found in the refrigerator. I guessed that Walter Westlake's monthly check had not yet arrived, and Ilse was attempting to keep the household going on credit. Steve's trip to Barcelona, from which he would presumably return with money available for borrowing, was indeed a momentous event.

Replacing the cook became a bark that relieved ennui, and as the Westlakes and their guests entered into the spirit of "playing serfs," the atmosphere became progressively lighter. All of us pitched in to set the table. Anita prepared the salad, Steve materialized two bottles of Cháteau d'Yquen, and there was uncustomary laughter and confusion as people darted in and out of the kitchen where Durward gave scientific attention to the ritual of preparing mushroom-and-shallot omelets.

After I had shooed Van Stuart from Denise's room and carried Denise's tray to her, I joined the others at the banquet-sized table. There, the unpretentious dinner, elegantly served by our proud chef, set the mood for a surprisingly convivial evening. Among the surprises was a toast to Denise's good health, proposed by Durward and enthusiastically echoed, even by Anita.

I excused myself early, aware of only one unpleasant note that marred the occasion: as they left the table, Steve and Anita seemed to be embroiled in a hushed but vicious argument of some kind. I caught only enough words to deduce that they were quarreling about money, and about Steve's "heartless rejection." Their arguments were so numerous that I would not have attached any significance to this one if I had not overheard Anita's hissing mention of Denise's name, her father's name . . . and mine.

At the time, knowing Anita's almost psychotic resentment of any woman whose bloom was still fresher than her own, I attached little importance to Steve's mocking laughter, or to the sentence, rising shrilly from Anita's throat and following me up the stairs: "Some day you will pay for your cruelty to me, Esteban! You will *all* suffer as you have made me suffer . . . you and Walter Westlake – that snip of a daughter of his, and that puerile American nurse you run after, making a fool of yourself. You will writhe in agony for your sins against me!"

Venomous words. Yet they meant no more, I thought, than catch phrases spewed out by a frustrated woman. How could I know that Anita's warning was prophetic . . . that a poison was already brewing in a caldron of hatred?

ELEVEN

Only Ilse and I were awake to see Steve Galvez off the next morning. He planned to drive to the airport outside Palma, leave his sports car parked there, and fly to Barcelona, pretending, for the benefit of his indulgent relative, that he had just returned from Paris.

Cheerful and radiantly handsome, in spite of what was for him "a positively obscene hour of the morning," Steve could not resist a final needle thrust at Ilse: "You see the sacrifices I make for you, dearest? Do nothing rash. Trusted Esteban will return, sober and covered with gold." He bent to kiss her forehead. "I have no doubt that you will have one hand out when I come back, Ilse. Remember that I will have been parched the entire time, *so*, in your other hand have ready a filled glass."

Ilse shook her head disparagingly, but she smiled. "If you were not so amusing, Steve, you would be utterly detestable."

Steve paused at the door of his car. "True.

I am totally corrupt." He flashed a brilliant grin at me, and then I saw the expression on his face change as rapidly as if a black cloud had obscured the sun. "As you may have discovered, Terecita, all of us here are rather worthless human beings. I have only one virtue." Steve's hand reached out to press mine warmly. He was not now the fearsome drunk who had forced himself upon me; I had the strange impression that he was a friend conveying a vital message to another. "In my corruption, I have the sole virtue of being harmless. This may not apply to ... everyone here."

Ilse's eyes followed him with a bewildered gaze as he drove off. I saw him make the turn near the foot of the hill, slow the car's motor for an instant, and turn back to wave. I waved back, blissfully ignorant of the circumstances under which I would hear of him again.

Steve and Craig Addison must have come within minutes of crossing paths at the airport. I was still trying to understand Steve's parting words to me when Craig arrived at the castle.

I was like a lovesick, nervous schoolgirl in his presence, awed by his nearness and thrilled by the subdued, resonant quality of his voice. But whatever hopeful daydreams I might have entertained about meeting Craig in a more romantic setting were dashed by the doctor's attitude. If anything, he was more impersonal and serious than before. He was deeply concerned about Denise, and in spite of tiredness from the hectic circumstances of his fast departure, he seemed obsessed with only one matter; to examine his patient and to determine whether or not he had erred in releasing her from his care.

Ilse had barely seen the doctor settled in a room just down the corridor from Denise's and mine, before he undertook his examination. And although he wanted to take Denise to a hospital where complete tests could be made, Craig was positive enough to announce his diagnosis in front of the patient.

"I don't detect any malfunction of the heart at all," he said.

Denise let out a triumphant whoop. "See, Terry? I told you there's nothing wrong with me."

Ilse breathed a deep sigh of relief. "We wanted to be cautious, darling. We had to obey the only doctor we had."

"I'll want to consult with him, of course," Craig said.

Ilse leaned over the bed to hug her niece. "I wanted the word of your own doctor, child.

Old Rivera has probably forgotten what little he ever learned in some second-rate school. Now we are certain that he was wrong, yes?"

While Craig still urged caution (for this patient's condition had mystified him once before), he gave his permission for Denise to go for a stroll along the beach with Van later that afternoon. Elated with the news, and bolstered by a check that arrived in the afternoon mail, Ilse decided to give an impromptu party for "neglected friends" the next evening. Reluctantly, it seemed, Anita Alma agreed to accompany Ilse on a shopping trip to Palma. I say "reluctantly," because Anita had quickly made it obvious that she considered the affluent American doctor an attractive prize.

Toward evening, with Durward locked in his study and ignoring the newest guest much as he ignored everyone else, I found myself alone with Craig. Self-conscious and awe-stricken (my usual condition under those circumstances), I offered to show him around the castle and the grounds. "Unless you'd . . . rather rest?" I said timidly.

He appeared to be preoccupied with his thoughts. "No, what I'd like to do – if you can spare the time – I'd appreciate your showing me where this Dr. Rivera can be reached."

I was more than willing to accompany Craig; a vague hope stirred inside me that the magic of the tiny Majorcan village would break down the doctor's reserve once more. Hadn't he kissed me once? After the visit with Dr. Rivera, there would be a long evening together in the most charming setting imaginable. There was always the possibility that Craig, too remembered that brief moment when he had held me in his arms.

In the old car that Craig had rented at the airport, we made our way to San Ysidro. I waited in Dr. Rivera's dingy reception-room-parlor while the two doctors consulted inside the office. Then, disappointingly, Craig turned the car back toward the castle, his mood hardly conducive to the romantic evening I had visualized.

Grim-faced behind the wheel, he gave his opinion of "old Rivera": "I'm convinced that the man is a conscientious and competent physician. He's kept careful records, and I have no reason to doubt that Denise *has* suffered cardiac irregularity." Craig shook his head. "Medically, it doesn't make sense."

He asked me a barrage of questions that might explain the mystery, yet there was only one conclusion to be reached: "I'm far from infallible. I found that out during Denise's first illness. She won't like this, but

109

I'm for getting her back to the hospital for observation."

I seized upon the idea with a revealing enthusiasm. "I was hoping you'd say that."

"Why?" Craig asked. "I should think you'd be terribly disappointed. Don't you like it here?"

How, without sounding like an utter fool, could I tell Craig Addison that I wanted to leave because I was afraid? Afraid of what? Rudi? He had not threatened me in any way. Because of Steve Galvez's sly hints? Durward's violent outburst of temper? These were not valid reasons. And Craig would have laughed at me if I had told him my fear was purely intuitive. "I just ... think your suggestion is sound, that's all," I lied. "Denise would probably be better off back home."

"Better off?" Craig asked. I glanced over at him to see an intense, inquiring light in his eyes. "Or safer?"

His question was left hanging as we arrived at the Castillo de los Tres Gatos. I had no concrete reply; no cause to arouse suspicion. Yet I was left with a baffling impression: Craig Addison suspected that Denise's heart irregularity had somehow been *induced*.

It was a thought that added uncertainty to an already discouraging evening – a thought that stabbed at me long after Denise had returned to her room, deliriously happy, and totally unaware that her doctor and her nurse were, once again, haunted by the possibility of her death.

TWELVE

Craig's unspoken suspicions and my own uneasiness came into the open the following afternoon.

Craig had been doing his utmost to avoid Anita, who had launched a blitzkrieg effort to win his attention. After he had turned down an invitation to play tennis with the ex-actress, he turned to me and said, "Could we go outside and talk, Terry?" He nodded graciously at Anita. "Professional consultation."

Anita's eyes bored through me with green fury as I walked out onto the rear terrace with Craig. Ironically, she might have had reason for resenting me, for Craig's "professional consultation" began with an emotion-stirring reminiscence. Looking out at the garden, with its background of palms and banana trees, he said, "It doesn't seem possible, does it, that a few months ago we were roughly three thousand miles away, looking out at a snow-covered city street. Do you remember the morning it was certain that Denise was out of the woods?"

I must have blushed, because Craig laughed gently. "I was almost drunk with success. I remember kissing you. I hope you haven't resented me for it."

"*Resented* you? Dr. Addison, I . . ."

"Craig," he said. "Please. We aren't observing protocol *this* far away from the hospital, are we?"

We had crossed the terrace to a secluded corner of the garden, and I was tense with a delicious anticipation. He had remembered. He had wanted to be alone with me now. Perhaps . . .

My hopes were shattered again as Rudi Gerhardt shuffled across the garden path on his way to the kitchen patio. He carried a pair of garden shears in his good hand. In his other hand he clutched a bouquet of freshly cut flowers.

Craig waited until he had passed. "Poor devil. I'd like five minutes with the butcher who did that mouth reconstruction. Walter told me it was a pathetic case."

I agreed with Craig's sympathetic comment, but my heart sank; the spell was gone and the subject had been changed. "He's picking flowers for Ilse's centerpiece. She's having guests tonight, you know. And Rudi's so anxious to please her."

"She's probably been very good to him and he's grateful," Craig said. There was an awkward silence, and then he waved at our surroundings. "He does an excellent job. I don't know one flower from another, but I can appreciate the effort that goes into keeping up a beautiful garden like this."

We had settled ourselves in lawn chairs, screened from the terrace by a wall of brilliant red-flowering hibiscus. "Well, you've just answered Esteban's question," I said. "He wondered if you were an expert in botany."

"Esteban?"

"Steve Galvez. A friend of Durward's. He's been a houseguest here . . . left yesterday morning. But he'll be back, and he said he's anxious to meet you."

"If he expects to discuss botany, he's in for a bad letdown." Craig smiled. "I'm city-bred. I just barely differentiate between dandelions and orchids. Why would he have assumed that I'm interested?"

"Oh . . . we were talking about . . . you know – Durward's favorite line of talk. Plants used for nefarious purposes. And Steve said he was sure you'd be interested in reading

113

some of Durward's books on the subject. He said . . . something about . . ." I paused, trying to recall Steve's exact words. "For one thing, he said you might be *curious*. Anyway, he's something of a lush. Clever, but . . ."

"Tell me exactly what he said," Craig demanded. He was suddenly alert, his expression more intense than I had ever seen it before.

As closely as I could recall it, I recounted the conversation that had taken place on the terrace two days ago. Craig listened attentively. Yet it was I, listening to my own words, who was overcome with the first shocking realization. "Steve talked about those spiked purple flowers over there, and he thought you'd be interested in reading some old book about them. They're called foxglove, and –" I stopped short, my eyes suddenly widening in horror. "Craig, how could I have missed what he was trying to say? Any nurse who's studied her pharmacy manuals knows what foxglove's used for."

"Digitalis," Craig murmured. "Acts on the heart muscle. We use it to slow the beat in a diseased heart. You cause the organ to empty more completely, and thus you increase the output."

Craig looked as stunned as I probably did, but we were both reluctant to express our thoughts. Finally, I put forth a tenous question. "If . . . someone was given a small dose of digitalis in its natural form, could that result in an erratic heartbeat and pulse?"

Craig's eyes were narrowed. "It would have to be carefully measured. The slightest overdose would be fatal."

"But the symptoms could be brought about that way? Say, in minute quantities?"

"Painstakingly measured quantities. Even a small amount would cause severe gastric pains and nausea."

"Dr. Rivera asked me about that," I blurted out. "So did Steve."

"If Denise showed any signs of gastric . . . ?"

"Yes! It must have occurred to them, Craig."

"That someone had given Denise digitalis?"

It was out. We were no longer sparring with words; the thought that we had both hesitated to express was in the open. "I said it would have had to be an expert," Craig reminded me. "Someone who knows the properties of the plant and the point at which it becomes toxic. That's making a gross accusation, Terry. It's like knowing *who*, without any idea of what was done, or why. What reason could there possibly be?"

We were silent again for a few moments,

and when Craig spoke again it was in a cautious half-whisper. "It's a terrible thought to entertain, isn't it? Like accusing a man, with only the flimsiest conjectures to go on. This . . . what was his name? Gomez?"

"Galvez," I corrected. "Steve Galvez."

"Did *he* ever suggest a possible motive?"

"Now that I think about it, he did nothing else *but*. But, Craig . . . if a man's income is doubled because his niece comes to stay with him, why would he want anything to happen to her? Durward has expensive tastes in books. His wife spends Walter Westlake's money as though it grew on trees, and Durward never seems to have enough for his research –"

"If the niece was suddenly to decide that she wants to leave," Craig interrupted, "wouldn't that upset the apple cart? Or if she fell in love and decided to get married, wouldn't that cut Walter's stipend in two again?"

"You mean . . . if Denise was kept a virtual invalid, he'd provide a meal ticket until –"

"Until Walter Westlake dies, and then she wouldn't be needed anymore. Denise is her father's principal heir – I know that." Craig caught a deep breath. "I also know who's second in line, Terry. It's Walter's only other relative. His brother." Craig let me ponder those facts for a few seconds and then, his tone free of its previous ominous quality, he said, "No, it doesn't add up. We're making unjust guesses to cover up for any inability to diagnose Denise's problem. Look, if someone wanted to use Denise as a meal ticket, the last thing he'd want would be a situation where her doctor would be summoned, right?"

My eyes met Craig's. "Didn't you wonder why I asked you to cable me in care of the Stuarts?"

"I wondered about it, yes. I sensed an urgency."

"Craig, I wrote to you. I left the letter for Durward to mail for me."

"I never received –"

"You never received it because it was destroyed. I found Rudi burning it with the trash."

Suddenly I was telling Craig every detail of the frightening things that had happened since my arrival at the castle – Durward's rage at finding me in his study, Rudi's burial of Denise's pet kitten, Steve's parting words to me: "In my corruption, I have the sole virtue of being harmless. This may not apply to . . . everyone here."

When I had finished, Craig was on his feet. "I've got to talk to Galvez. Would you know where to reach him?"

"He's staying with an aunt in Barcelona," I said. "I only know her first name, but we could ask —"

"We can't ask *anyone* here," Craig said sharply. "Think. Would anyone in the village . . . ?"

"There's only a faint possibility that Dr. Rivera's heard the name. He and Steve had several conversations here when the doctor came to see Denise. We could try to locate a Victoria Galvez, but if she's a relative on Steve's *mother's* side, her name wouldn't be . . ."

"We'll try Rivera first," Craig said. "Meanwhile, don't say anything to anyone here. We could be completely wrong, Terry. A rather unforgivable way to repay the Westlakes' hospitality."

I nodded. "Especially considering Steve's personality. He drinks too much and he has a flair for cloak-and-dagger melodrama. I mean, he likes throwing out subtle little barbs that turn people against each other." I reflected for a moment. "Besides, he shares Durward's interest in plants. He's Durward's friend. That conversation about foxglove could have been perfectly natural."

Craig was guiding me back toward the terrace, listening to my arguments, it seemed, with only half an ear. Did my apologia sound

118

as hollow to him as it sounded to me? His jaw was set in a grim line as he repeated, "We'll try Rivera first."

THIRTEEN

Francisco Rivera not only knew the name of Steve's aunt; he had been familiarized with some of her less endearing aspects. In the musty room outside his office, a quarters which brought to the nostrils an amalgam of moldy bricks, ether, and sea salt, the pot-bellied man who wore the fluffy white halo blinked his flesh-bound eyes and said, "*Sí*, Esteban is told me . . . she is the sister of his father. Who calls this woman a religious fanatic? If you can believe it, the Archbishop of her diocese, *he* is the one who calls her this!" Rivera's eyes twinkled at the thought. "She treats to leave her money to a convent, so you understand, *Señor, Doctor*, as a friend you will please not reveal that Esteban has been here to live a life with dissolution."

Craig assured the old doctor that we had no intention of shaking Steve's position with his super-virtuous relative. "We only want to ask him a few questions," Craig explained.

Satisfied that his countryman's confidences would not be betrayed, Dr. Rivera added, "So fascinating a man, Galvez, no? How my heart is broke to see this greatest intelligence go . . ." He made a downward gesture with his hands, indicating talent going down the drain.

Then, as further proof that we had come to the right source, Rivera told us that his was one of the few telephones in San Ysidro. Furthermore, since a certain technique and a long training in patience were required if there was to be any service at all, he would volunteer to place the call. It was the old doctor's polite way of telling us that before we reached Steven Galvez, we would have to communicate in our flimsy Spanish with an operator and probably an uncomprehending old woman in Barcelona.

Twenty minutes later, his calm unruffled where any American would have exploded in frustration, Dr. Rivera was speaking in rapid fire Castilian to someone on the other end of the line. Waiting expectantly, Craig and I watched the doctor's heavy-jowled face lose its color. A shocked expression came into his eyes, and I understood enough of what he was saying to realize that something was drastically wrong.

"Ay Dios, que lástima, señorita! En qué hospital esta? Qué dicen los doctores?"

What did the doctors say? In which hospital was he? Oh, God, what a shame! What had happened?

It seemed that eons had gone by before Dr. Rivera dropped the receiver. He turned toward us, sorrow clouding his features, revealing what I had already surmised: Esteban Galvez had been taken to a hospital in Barcelona.

"Poor woman, she is in hysterical, so great are her grief," Rivera said. From what he had gathered, Steve had been seized by violent internal pains only a few hours ago. His Aunt Victoria had accompanied him to the hospital, and had left his side only long enough to rush home for a rosary that had been blessed by a Pope; Dr. Rivera had caught her in the act of hurrying out of the house, and she had been barely able to speak, convinced that the call was from the hospital, reporting Steve's death.

Dr. Rivera didn't have to be asked. Minutes later he was trying to reach a former colleague in the Barcelona hospital. After another seemingly endless period he was able to give us some of the details. "The pain have subsided to some degrees," he said. He expected that the patient was under sedation.

"But what's the diagnosis?" Craig asked.

"To begin, all symptoms are indicating

121

poison. But now it is believed *no*." Dr. Rivera added that a check of the patient's meals over the past twenty-four hours, and an analysis of the stomach contents, had ruled out the possibility of any toxic substance. There was, regrettably, a marked hardening of the liver. *"Pobre Esteban!"* The old doctor shook his head. "Often do I tell him to not drink, drink, drink!"

Craig's eyes locked with mine. "You told me he couldn't leave liquor alone. You know what Dr. Rivera's saying, don't you, Terry?"

"Cirrhosis of the liver?" I guessed. "But he is still in his thirties."

Dr. Rivera had begun pacing his cluttered office. "Yes. And never before is he sick. So sudden this onset, no? So violent. It makes to wonder."

Craig nodded slowly. "Yes. Yes, it does."

It makes to wonder. Were Dr. Rivera and Craig considering the same insidious thought that persisted even though poisoning had been dismissed as a cause for Steve's excruciating pains, even though a logical explanation existed. Steve had made a joke of the fact that he was sober only during his mercenary pilgrimages to Barcelona; inevitably the prolonged consumption of alcohol could have damaged an organ without which man cannot exist. Appalling as this was, why did

122

my imagination have to reach beyond these facts? Had I grown so paranoid that I conjured up evil where none existed?

Although Craig was almost as shaken by this development as I was, and although Dr. Rivera had evidently established a warmer rapport with Steve than I had realized, so that the news saddened him personally, we lingered on for a while, observing the amenities that are demanded by Spanish custom. It would have been unthinkable to dash in, American style, ask a favor of our host, and then, business concluded, rush off.

We talked about a variety of unrelated subjects, but always in somber, hushed tones, the way strangers speak when they have heard of another's tragedy. Dr. Rivera was curious about Craig's training, about the hospital in New York, about new techniques and recent developments in the medical field. He was interested, too, in my work as a nurse, none of his questions aimed at satisfying idle curiosity, but intellectual probes from which he obviously hoped to learn more about his profession.

When we finally drew him out, so that he told us something about himself, we learned that he was far from being the uninformed country bumpkin Ilse Westlake had imagined him to be. In 1936, he had been at the peak of a brilliant career as an internist in Madrid. A Spanish Republican, he had sent his wife and two children to what he believed was the safety of his parents' home in the provinces, and enlisted his services in the medical corps. Francisco Rivera's loss in the battle against Fascist forces was compounded by a more personal heartbreak. During the war, shells had demolished the cottage in which his family were living, and they were killed.

Persecuted for his political views, torn by grief, he had courageously buried one life and somehow started another, devoting his medical knowledge to the care of the often impoverished villagers of San Ysidro.

Tears glistened in the old doctor's eyes when he had finished telling his story. It had been told with humility; the fact that we were in the presence of a distinguished and selfless physician came through in spite of his unaffected modesty. When Craig and I took our leave of the man, we knew that he was a man to be trusted, and a doctor whose reports on Denise could not be questioned.

It was because we understood this about him, because we knew that he would not stoop to subterfuge except in the cause of a just principle, that Craig and I were stunned by his parting words: "It would be for better if nothing is said to others of Esteban's misfortune, no? We will observe. We wait. Then, perhaps, we know."

As we drove back to the castle, we were silent for a long time, each of us locked in private thought. Finally I asked, "Why do you think Dr. Rivera didn't want us to tell anyone about Steve? Durward's his friend; isn't it logical that he'd want to know?"

"Why do you think?" Craig challenged.

It was difficult to express my conclusion. I phrased it as another question. "Does he think Steve's attack might not be . . . natural?"

Craig turned the rented sedan around a steep curving grade before he replied. "Rivera's no fool, Terry. He asked some pointed questions about Denise's condition yesterday. He may have his suspicions, but he can hardly come out and announce them. For example, he didn't ask you how Steve Galvez was feeling when he left here. Let me ask you that now."

My answer should have ended any wild conclusions about foul play. "He was in excellent health . . . exceptionally good spirits," I said. "Craig, I'm beginning to feel rotten about the way I've let a few unpleasant incidents poison my thinking. Mentally, I've practically accused Durward of attempted murder. With only the flimsiest evidence and, in Steve's case, absolutely no motive. Is it the atmosphere in that gloomy place that's warping my perspective? I keep remembering something I heard Anita say to Steve the night before he left. Something about making him suffer, the way he's allegedly made *her* suffer. I'm attaching ugly implications to everything. I'm . . . beginning to reason like a witch-hunter. Really, Craig, it's despicable."

Craig didn't disagree. Nevertheless, neither of us said anything about Steve Galvez that evening. Craig was roped into joining the Westlakes and Anita as they hosted a small group of Ilse's expatriate friends at dinner; I used Denise as a pretext to excuse myself from the dull affair. I lingered downstairs long enough to meet a retired German colonel and his shrill wife, a pair of "artists" who had been pointed out to me by Steve as "studied bohemian phonies," and a middle-aged *nouveau riche* couple from New Jersy who had "made a killing in the plumbing line," and whose culture seemed suited to their calling. Ilse was quite impressed with each member of this unhomogenous gathering, fluttering about them like the proverbial social butterfly, while Anita, dramatic in black velvet, concentrated on Craig. The expected dinner conversation held little promise for me, and I was too disturbed about Steve's illness to force myself into a party mood.

"What a pity you cannot stay," Anita cooed. "We are all going to drive to Palma after dinner. Mr. Singletary" – she cast a seductive glance at the paunchy ex-plumber – "has promised to treat us to a divine new club where gypsy music is featured." Linking her arm through Craig's, Anita turned her back on me. "Do you like gypsy music, darling? I am such a romantic fool – my heart beats *insanely* when I hear violins cry. And so it will be good to have a clever doctor at my side, do you agree?"

I hadn't heard about the after-dinner plans. (In any event, I would not have been included because Denise couldn't be left alone in the castle with a newly hired cook, two ignorant housemaids, and Rudi.) Now, to my already depressed state was added the knowledge that Craig would be away half the night in the company of a determined and rather dazzling woman.

Van Stuart had been kept from visiting Denise by some minor family obligation at home, leaving me to play a poor substitute. Fortunately, it was difficult to converse with Denise about anything *but* Van, and I was relieved of the problem of avoiding less pleasant subjects.

By eleven o'clock, Denise was beginning to yawn. Tiredness, however, didn't inhibit her happy chatter. She rattled on in her usual slangy, carefree vein; yet there were two moments that made me shudder inwardly. The first came when Denise said, "I wonder if old sousepot's managing to stay dry in Barcelona. Y'know, I *like* Steve. You have to know him a while, and you have to ignore a few bad habits, but, like Van says, he's a real swinger. He's so sharp, and ... I dunno ... for an adult, he's so *alive*."

I had to pretend interest in a pot of ferns near the window to hide my reaction. Later, I turned away to pretend the same absorption in an oil portrait on the wall when Denise asked peevishly, "I wonder if somebody *swiped* V.L.Y.? Van says kittens never go very far, so he's sure it'll turn up either here or at his place, but ... I have a hunch somebody adopted it, y'know? I mean, it's such a cute, lively little thing, anybody'd just love it to death."

The beautiful Spanish lady of the portrait stared down at me with dark melancholy eyes. I wondered about her, as I wondered about every female whose image graced the walls of the castle – was she the one who had also been fond of cats?

Through the open window came the sound

of laughter and exuberant conversation. An automobile motor started up, then a car was heard roaring down the grade. It was followed by another, and then a third; Ilse's party leaving for the night club in Palma. Craig was gone. The only man in the castle was Rudi Gerhardt.

Denise was having trouble keeping her eyes open. I wondered how I could go to my room without cautioning her to lock her door from the inside. To do so would have brought on a barrage of questions; vague replies would have frightened her.

While I was combing my mind for a solution to this dilemma, Denis fell asleep. I would spend the night in her room, I decided. I would . . .

Someone was walking in the hallway outside the door.

I held my breath until my lungs threatened to explode.

Heavy, masculine footsteps. Rudi! Was he stopping?

I reached for the lock, startled by the loud rattle of its antiquated mechanism as I turned it. In the stillness of the dark corridor, the sound must have echoed like gunfire. The footsteps had stopped, and the only sound now was the desperate thumping of my heart.

Was he standing outside the door? Was he flexing that horribly mutilated hand, waiting to . . .

"Is that you, Terry? Are you still awake?"

I nearly sobbed with relief. It was Craig's voice, hushed, but clearly recognizable. My fingers shook convulsively as I undid the lock, then opened the door. As I stepped into the corridor, tense nerves gave way and I released the suppressed cry within me. "Oh, Craig, I was so afraid . . ."

Had I stumbled forward into his arms, or had they closed around me? For a quiet eternity I clung to Craig, his arms holding me protectively.

Then, embarrassed, I moved away from him and stammered, "I . . . thought it was . . . Rudi."

"He's fast asleep," Craig said quietly. "I checked before I came up here."

"Are the others back, too?"

"I didn't go." Craig's faint smile was vaguely reminiscent of Steve's, when the latter had infuriated Anita Alma in the same way. "I wasn't about to leave you and Denise here alone. That was one reason."

"You had another?" I asked.

"Besides wanting to escape from that female vampire?" Craig glanced toward the stairway, as if to make certain he wasn't being overheard. "I wanted a look at Mr Westlake's library. I didn't think Ilse would get him out of the place, but she managed it somehow. Trouble is, I . . . don't want to get caught snooping. I thought if you were still awake, you might . . . stand guard." Craig smiled. "Watch for cars coming up the hill. You remember the old gangster movies? The gun moll keeping an eye open for the law while the mob blew open a bank safe?"

In spite of my nervousness, I couldn't help laughing. "You don't look like a thug. What are you going to do, steal Durward's first editions?"

"No, I think it's called casing the joint. You can say no, and I won't mind, Terry. It's not a nice thing I'm going to do. Let's just say your friend Galvez had me properly pegged. I'm curious."

"What about Denise?"

"I told you . . . Rudi's out like a light and there's no one else here. She'll be perfectly safe."

I closed the door to Denise's room quietly. As we walked toward the stairway, I couldn't resist asking, "Do you think she might *not* be safe, Craig? Is that what you're thinking?"

"I don't want to frighten you," was Craig's reply. "I only want to be cautious."

131

"But you think . . ."

"If my hunch is correct, we aren't safe, either," Craig said. "Your friend Galvez might not have been safe."

A few minutes later we were inside Durward's library, a bit chagrined, in our role as spies, to have discovered the door unlocked. Craig had started examining the shelves, and as I started toward a window that afforded an excellent view of the road leading upward to the castle, he called to me. "This is interesting, Terry. Look."

I hesitated. "I'd better watch."

"Oh, they won't be home for hours," Craig said. "Look at this."

I crossed the dimly lighted room to where Craig stood, a small, ancient-looking book with a tattered gray cloth cover held open in his hand.

"I don't know if it was instinct that made me reach for this one first, or . . . seeing that the dust was smeared on the shelf. Someone's evidently looked at this book very recently." Craig held the open volume so that I could read the page to which it had been opened. "Can you see these tiny ink checks? Look at the margin."

I strained my eyes to find the marks Craig

was pointing out to me. As small as they were, it was evident that they were freshly made, the blue ink checks unfaded and clearly defined. Then, reading the text, which an archaic type face and inadequate light made difficult, I said, "It's an encyclopedia of poisonous plants, Craig."

" 'Nightshade,' " Craig read aloud. "That's belladonna – and there's a mark after the listing. *'The source of a virulent and nerve paralyzing poison.'* Here's another; *'Foxglove, known to the ancients as the Queen Mother of Poisons.'* Complete with a full description and . . . recipes."

Craig thumbed through several more pages. Wherever one of the pen marks followed the name of a flower, it was invariably one of the plants Steve Galvez had talked about so incisively his last afternoon at the castle.

"These are the plants Steve talked about," I said. "Craig, do you suppose he –"

I gasped, leaving my sentence unfinished as the room was flooded with light.

"A priceless collector's item," Durward's voice said, "and historically interesting, but totally useless in my research."

I spun around to see Durward Westlake standing in the doorway to the hothouse, his hand still on the light switch. I could think of nothing to say, nothing to explain this

133

second intrusion, and I steeled myself for a repeated outburst of violent anger. Instead, the gawky figure in rumpled tweeds walked toward us casually. In a calm, nonchalant tone, as though it were perfectly natural to find strangers in his library, Durward said, "I had hoped you would share my interest in botany, Doctor. My friend Steve Galvez suggested that you might."

Craig managed to appear completely at ease. "Interest doesn't imply knowledge, I'm afraid. But I'm tremendously impressed by your collection."

Durward barely glanced in my direction. "I'm proud of it," he acknowledged. "Always delighted to share it with a scientifically oriented person who appreciates its value. Most people don't, you know. I shudder at having them touch some of these rare volumes." I felt my face color as he added, "I'm inclined to lose my temper when I find my library being used as a menagerie for wayward pets."

His hands surprisingly steady, Craig replaced the volume we had been examining. "You're very gracious. I feel something of an intruder."

"Not at all, not at all," Durward insisted. "I'm sure you haven't been told that the library is off limits to you. But if you're interested in my field, you might enjoy examining some of the more recent, more comprehensive studies." He indicated the check-marked book with a wave of his long arm. "I gave that volume a cursory glance some years ago. It has no value except as a curiosity. Here –" he pointed at a row of newer looking volumes in fresh dust jackets. "Here you will find the most recent data on the clinical uses of plants that were known to the ancients and are only now beginning to be recognized by modern scientists."

As I slowly began to recover from my shock, gradually assured that Durward was actually *pleased* to have a qualified man of science interested in his library, my legs stopped shaking and I was able to at least imitate Craig's self-controlled manner. Encouraged by an attentive audience, Durward went on, carried away by his subject.

"Read about snakeroot, Doctor, for an insight into the blind stupidity of your predecessors in medicine. Yes, snakeroot. *Rauwolfia*. For centuries, this astounding root was used in the Orient in the treatment of disturbed minds. Yet the very concept was pooh-poohed as primitive mumbo-jumbo, even when two East Indian chemists extracted the active ingredient and demonstrated its positive effects in the treatment of insanity. Witchcraft, they were told. Old wives' tales. The chemists were fortunate in that they were ignored; usually such heretical scientists are persecuted or, at best, jeered out of their profession. Then, years wasted, and finally science catches up to the shaman, to the witch doctor. *Rauwolfia* is now a preferred treatment for hypertension. More research, now that the ridicule has stopped. And from the snakeroot our scientifical pundits extract the chemical fraction you undoubtedly know as reserpine, Doctor. Out, electroconvulsive therapy; in, the age of tranquilizers. An age that snakeroot opened in the Orient twenty-five hundred years ago!"

Durward had started pacing the room, enthusiasm for his subject taking on the form of physical agitation. "Natives in the jungles of Peru and Bolivia, in Colombia and Brazil, were using the leaves of the coco shrub for untold centuries before Koller discovered the use of cocaine as an anesthetic in eye operations. The Indians were 'superstitious savages'; *we* had educated opthalmologists! It took us until the nineteenth century to learn what every bareskinned Peruvian had known from birth.

"Today we stand in awe before the consciousness-expanding drugs, drugs capable of changing the minds of men for good or for evil purposes, of giving the consciousness a key to the very meaning of life. What pious Aztec priest was unfamiliar with Teonanácatl, the magic mushroom we call *psilocybe Mexicana?* We have 'discovered' mescaline; American Indians in our own Southwest had long before constructed a sophisticated religion around the hallucinogenic button of the peyote cactus. And centuries before the LSD controversy exploded in our laboratories, ergot, the rye fungus, was sweeping Europe with the 'dancing madness' in which entire villages danced themselves into insensibility." Durward paused. "I defeat my own argument with ergot. The properties of ergot caused this devastation precisely because they were *un*known. At least to the uninitiated peasant. However, there was undoubtedly a knowledgeable sorcerer watching the spectacle from the side-lines."

Durward continued, uninterrupted, for at least half an hour. We were acquainted with the toxic qualities of some of the least suspected plants or portions of plants; simple English ivy, seeds of the lovely wisteria, foliage of such delectable innocents as figs, walnuts, and cherries, the latter containing a compound that released cyanide and proved fatal when consumed. I was amazed to discover that the leaf blade of rhubarb contained an equally virulent poison, while the stalk was not merely edible but delicious.

It was like listening to a walking encyclopedia of little-known botanical facts – knowledge that had influenced mankind, as Durward phrased it, "for better or for worse." In my fascination, I had forgotten Craig's objective in coming to the library.

Finally, it was our host who ended the visit. "Browse at will," he invited. "I must get back to watering my flats . . . some illustrations for my book that I want to photograph. Can't get pictures if nothing sprouts for lack of water." He started back toward the hothouse. "I was nearly induced into wasting an entire evening. Fortunately, I remembered that I hadn't taken care of the moisture problem before we got too far. Ilse is probably still upset about my demanding that she stop the car. She's convinced that I'm too decrepit to walk a few hundred yards uphill."

That explained Durward's presence; he had evidently returned to the castle on foot, unnoticed by Craig. Yet after Craig and I had said good night to Durward, lingering in the library and faking a loud conversation that, hopefully, removed us from suspicion, we couldn't help wondering if the lecture had been a diversionary tactic.

As we climbed the stairs, Craig whispered, "He may have wanted to distract us from that marked book by dismissing it as puerile. The object could have been to impress us with his superior knowledge, so that we wouldn't think he'd been reading about the more obvious poisonous drugs."

"That's one possibility," I agreed. "But suppose he was sincere, Craig? Someone else might have been interested in the uses of foxglove. Anita might have reason to do some . . . research. Even Ilse. We can't make accusations. It might have been innocent curiosity." I thought for a few seconds. "The information seemed rather elementary to be of interest to Steve, but . . . it's almost as though he had been *quoting* from it."

At my door, Craig stopped and said, "Then, there's the final possibility; that we've blown a few puzzling incidents into a macabre mystery. As you say, Galvez left this place in good shape. Denise may have overexerted herself; she's fine now. I think we have more appealing subjects to discuss."

He was looking at me intently, and

suddenly my heart was pounding again, but not from fear.

"On second thought, words might be superfluous," Craig said. His arms reached out to pull me close to him. "I've waited so long to say this that words won't suffice, Terry. It doesn't seem enough just to say 'I love you.' I've been afraid of love. I . . . don't think I have to be afraid anymore. Do I?"

He bent to kiss me, and the joyous warmth of my response was all the answer he needed. There were no words necessary between us; we let our nearness to each other speak for itself.

Then, almost giddy with happiness, I embraced Craig and laughed as he said, "So much time to make up for, and we've been wasting it, in this beautiful place, playing comic book detectives! Trying to read something sinister into the actions of a houseful of oddballs and a guy who's evidently determined to drink himself to death."

"That was silly, tonight," I agreed. "Spying on an eccentric amateur botanist . . . the sort of kook who'd spend I-don't-know-how-many years writing a book maybe five people are going to buy. That's what Denise said." I giggled as Craig planted a playful kiss on the tip of my nose. "I think I remember the name of it. It's a jawbreaker." Facetiously,

I pronounced the title in pompous tones: *"Aspects of Herbology and Mycology in Relation to Medieval Witchcraft Practices in Central and Southern Europe."*

Craig's muscles stiffened, and he released me. "Did you say *mycology?*"

"Uhuh. I hate to admit it, but I don't know what it means. Is it an obsolete term for the study of microbes, or . . . ?"

"Mushrooms," Craig whispered. "Mycology . . . the study of fungi! I looked over into the hothouse and I didn't think of it at the time, but those were mushroom trays Durward was watering. Poisonous mushrooms, probably."

"That's not unusual, is it? It fits in with his field of interest." I looked up to see a contemplative scowl on Craig's face. "What are you thinking?"

He ran a hand over his forehead. "I don't know. Maybe you're right, Terry. I'm beginning to see villainy in the most innocuous facts. I'll get so paranoid, I'll be afraid to eat beef stroganoff if it's served here."

"As a matter of fact," I remembered, "We had mushrooms with eggs the night before Steve left. All of us. With no bad results, even though that ogre downstairs did the cooking."

"Durward?"

"Yes. But I happen to know that the

mushrooms were bought in the village market – they didn't come from the hothouse of . . . of one of those mad scientists you see in cheap horror films." I shook my head in self-disgust. "Let's stop this sort of conjecture, Craig, please. I'm so happy now, I . . . I don't want any negative thinking to spoil it."

We had decided, before our final good-night kiss, to stop weaving diabolical plots around our host and the other people living at the Castillo. We had made a thrilling discovery about each other; we were in love, and in this dream-come-true there was no room for imaginary nightmares.

A new kind of day would dawn for me tomorrow – a day filled with the promise of Craig's love. Why, when there was no concrete evidence to bolster it, why destroy this beautiful idyll with groundless suspicion of intended murder?

FOURTEEN

It was not fear that kept me awake that night. I lay sleepless, knowing it was true, yet somehow unable to believe that the incredible had happened; Craig loved me.

142

Except for the intermittent chirping of crickets, and the soft bell-like tinkling of the fountain below my window, the night was deathly still. Restless, I got up from my bed and crossed the room to look down into the garden. The scene was one of exquisite peace and beauty. Moonlight filtered through the palms to draw a lacy pattern of light and shadow across the velvet lawn. Under the ethereal light, blossoms of white oleander formed a galaxy of stars against the somber foliage, and through the window there drifted the faint perfume of orange blossoms. It was a night that would have inspired love even in a soul where no love had ever existed before.

My ecstatic mood was short-lived. As I gazed at the dreamlike setting, a shadow moved. I concentrated on the dark patch beside the rose garden; surely I was mistaken! The long shadow moved again. Incredulous, I made out the dim shadow of a man, grotesquely elongated, as was the stick he seemed to be wielding. After a while, I deduced that it must be Rudi, the image of his squat body stretched to giant proportions by the light's angle. The shadow was not standing still; the thing it held was a shovel, and whoever it was, was digging in the spot where Rudi had buried Denise's dead kitten!

I had a momentary impulse to run down the

hall and knock on Craig's door. He would be interested in knowing why Rudi or Durward (the long shadow suggested our lanky host) would be digging in the rose garden at that hour of the night.

Before I could coordinate my thoughts with actions, twin headlights rose like fiery suns from the foot of the hill. As Ilse's car came into view, the figure behind the rose bed darted out of sight behind a huge magnolia tree. A few seconds later the car crunched up the gravel driveway; doors slammed, and I heard Ilse and Anita talking in the loud whispers people use when they are aware that others nearby are sleeping.

I heard the two women come up the stairs shortly afterward, their high heels clicking a staccato duet across the tiled corridor. Doors opened and closed; then silence settled over the castle once more.

Whoever had been in the garden . . . was *still* in the garden . . . had obviously wanted to avoid being seen. I kept watch over the magnolia tree, breathing hard, convinced that the mysterious man with the shovel was still in his hiding place.

My guess was correct. After an interminable wait at the window, someone stepped out from behind the tree. At first, his form obscured by the black outline of hedges, pressing himself against the protective darkness of a low adobe wall, the man was no more identifiable than his shadow. Then, as he stepped into the open moonlit area between the rose garden and the terrace, his features were plainly visible.

I drew an astonished breath. Moving surreptitiously, a small canvas bag dangling from one hand, the man hurried toward the concealment of the rear terrace. He had evidently discarded the shovel. Minutes later I heard footsteps on the stairway again, more cautious footsteps in the hall, a door at the end of the corridor opening and closing softly. My mind reeled. The man I had seen in the garden was Craig Addison!

Sleep was impossible now. I lay in bed, alternately chilled and feverish, struggling to cope with this puzzling new development. This was surely paranoid madness; as desperately as I tried to shut out the thoughts, I could not escape the insidious seeds of distrust that had been planted in my mind. Did Craig have reason to see Denise out of the way? He had assured me she was in good health – actually encouraged exercise and a normal pattern of activities. Had he known that there was something wrong with her heart? He was Walter Westlake's close friend. Was he, perhaps, next in line of succession in the advertising executive's will, following Denise and Durward Westlake? If so, it would be natural for him to cast doubt on Durward's character. Now, again, he had assured everyone that Denise was recovered. But was she? Had he rushed to Majorca not because Denise was ill but because she had survived an expected heart attack?

Ugly, consuming thoughts, befouling my trust in a man I loved and would always love – a man who had offered his love to me. Was it poison in the very atmosphere of Castillo de los Tres Gatos that had seeped into my consciousness? Once before, within these walls, a woman had loved in blind faith. Her body had been sealed into thick masonry walls exactly like those that threatened to close in on me now. Her skeleton would have remained in its gray sepulchre except for the piteous yowling of . . .

I had heard it! It wasn't imagined; I had heard the piteous yowling of a cat!

The sound was cut off abruptly. I sat up in bed, suddenly damp with icy perspiration. Immobile with fear, I sat listening, straining all my senses, but there was no further noise.

Mercifully, exhaustion overcame my tense nerves. I had drifted into a troubled sleep, for I was not fully conscious when I heard the indistinct sound of someone running through the corridor. As awareness flooded over me, I realized that the sun was just beginning to peep over the horizon; no one except Rudi Gerhardt would be awake at that hour. The shuffling gait of those footsteps confirmed my guess. Rudi. Why would he be up here at daybreak? Why, unless . . . ?

Suddenly frantic, I leaped out of bed, pausing only long enough to throw a robe over my shoulders.

There was no one in the corridor. But as I approached Denise's room I saw that the door was slightly open. I knew it had been closed when I checked on Denise earlier. Was someone in her room?

As I approached the door, a shrill scream from inside the room froze my blood. I didn't think to call for help. I burst into the room, expecting to find Rudi bending over the girl's bed. Instead, I almost collided with Denise as I rushed in.

"What is it?" I cried. "Are you all right?"

She was standing near the doorway, clad only in her nightgown, a look of indescribable horror distorting her pretty face. Her eyes were focused on an object that lay at her feet; in her hand was a dirty burlap bag which she held away from her body as though it were a loathsome thing, yet which she was too shocked to hurl away from her.

"Denise, what . . ."

She whimpered, and I followed her gaze to the tiled floor. Sprawled in a grotesque position, its head twisted as though someone had wrung its neck, was a dead black cat.

"Where did that come from?" I asked. "Denise, come over here. Stop staring at it."

I led her away from the door. She was almost numb with shock. "I . . . heard the door open," Denise whispered. "Someone . . . shoved *this* into the room." She dropped the burlap bag as though she had just become aware of it. "I got out of bed. I . . . picked the bag up . . ." She grabbed at my wrist, fingernails digging into my flesh in a desperate attempt to fight back hysteria. "The cat rolled out. It's dead! Somebody . . ."

Denise's voice had risen to a shrill, uncontrollable pitch. She was gasping for breath, and her eyes blazed with a wild light. I was shaking myself, but I forced myself to stay calm. "Lie down and take it easy, honey," I said. "It's only . . ."

There were no words to explain the gruesome episode. Denise's eyes met mine as I led her to her bed. "Why?" she asked. "Why, Terry? Why would anybody do such a terrible thing?" She gasped as someone knocked on the door.

"Denise? May I come in?" It was Craig.

148

I patted Denise's arm. "Easy now." In a louder voice, I called, "Come in."

Craig stepped into the room, his eyes still heavy with sleep. He wore a look of puzzled concern. "I thought I heard . . ." His eyes found the gruesome black bundle on the floor. "What's this? What's going on here, Terry?"

He had left the door open behind him, and his question was echoed almost instantly by Anita Alma's voice. "What's the trouble? Is someone ill?"

Amazingly, Anita looked as though she were made up for a special occasion. Had she been awake at this hour? Anita, who never stirred from her bed before noon? True, she had probably been aroused by Denise's scream, but if she had really been asleep, would she be appearing now with every fold of her black satin lounging pajamas, every hair of her elegant coiffure, in place? Hating Denise as she did, obsessed with getting revenge for Walter Westlake's rejection of her, would Anita have been capable of paying Rudi to terrify Denise in the hope of inducing a heart attack? And had she come into the room now to gloat over her success?

"There's nothing wrong," I told Anita curtly. "Denise was having a bad dream and . . ."

149

My excuse, used in the hope of getting rid of Anita and calming Denise, fell flat as Anita gasped. "What is *this?* Ohh! Oh, how *dreadful!* This ugly thing . . . what is it doing here? Oh, it is dead! Craig, what is the meaning . . . ?"

Anita's reaction to the cat's body was more severe than Denise's. Overcome with horror, she threatened my patient with an infectious hysteria. I couldn't help feeling grateful as Craig took the woman's arm and guided her out of the room. She looked positively ill.

"Denise is somewhat upset now," Craig said softly. "We'll talk about it later, Anita." He thanked her for her concern, and seconds afterward he returned, closing the door behind him. While I talked soothingly to Denise, Craig left the room again, this time removing the cat and the burlap bag in which it had been delivered. He came back once more with a sedative tablet for Denise.

We made no guesses as to how or why the grisly package had been shoved into Denise's quarters. "Some moron's idea of a practical joke," was all Craig said. He checked Denise's pulse and, with me, sat quietly near the bed until the sedative took effect. Daylight had flooded the room before Denise finally closed her eyes and slept. I envied her that drugged oblivion.

Outside the room, Craig turned to me and half whispered, "I'm sorry, Terry. I couldn't explain it to Denise, but I'm afraid I'm to blame for what happened."

"*You?*"

Speaking in a tone that would not be audible behind any of the doors lining the corridor, Craig said, "Last evening I asked Rudi to dig up the other kitten you told me about, the one you'd seen him burying in the rose garden."

"You asked him . . ." I shook my head uncomprehendingly. "But why?"

"I told him I wanted it for an experiment." Craig hesitated. "I didn't tell him I wanted to have it autopsied. At any rate, he didn't oblige."

I was having an increasingly difficult time understanding Craig. "He probably didn't bring it to you because he was afraid of being scolded. I'm sure he strangled the poor thing."

"I'm already certain that he *didn't*," Craig said. "When he went to sleep without bringing the kitten's body to me, I did a little digging in a spot where the ground had been disturbed recently. What's left of Denise's Siamese is in my room. And my guess is that it died of an internal problem. No broken bones, no evidence of strangulation."

Craig darted a glance down the hall. "Let's walk over toward the stairway, Terry. I don't want anyone tuning in on this."

Completely out of earshot of any possible eavesdropper, Craig went on, "The teeth are exposed in the kind of agonized death grimace associated with excruciatingly painful poisoning. I'm taking it to Dr. Rivera later, in the morning . . . asking him for an analysis of the stomach contents. So far, my hunch is still holding up."

I was sickened by the thought that I had constructed a diabolical plot out of Craig's actions in the garden. He held no secrets from me; it was shameful for me to have mistrusted him. "What hunch?" I asked.

"I remembered reading somewhere that European peasants used to test wild mushrooms by feeding them to kittens. I . . . haven't been able to stop thinking about Steve Galvez. Wondering if . . . someone used a kitten for a guinea pig."

"To make sure a certain type of mushroom was poisonous?" I thought about that fiendish possibility for a moment and then dismissed it. "An idea like that wouldn't occur to anyone but Durward. And he wouldn't have to test. He'd *know*."

"It does sound far-fetched," Craig admitted. "Especially since Steve wasn't sick immediately after that dinner you spoke of. And since all of you ate the same meal. What was it you said? Scrambled eggs with mushrooms, right?"

It was as though a lightning bolt had struck my brain. Why hadn't I thought of it before? "Craig, we had *omelets!* Individually prepared omelets! Durward fixed them in order of our seating at the table."

Craig released a low-keyed whistle. "Then *one* of them could have been different from the others. Did anyone else have access to the kitchen during this process?"

"All of us, except Denise," I said. "Anita, Steve, Ilse. Put me on the suspect list. I was in and out of the kitchen half a dozen times while the meal was being prepared. Craig, it doesn't make sense! Durward and Steve were good friends. Even if someone else doctored up Steve's omelet with poisonous mushrooms, he'd have recognized the fact. The taste, the smell, a different appearance. Steve would have known the difference. Remember, he knows almost as much about Durward's field of study as Durward himself. In fact, it was the basis for their friendship. Durward doesn't get close to people who can't talk to him about his favorite subject on his own level."

Craig shrugged. "You're probably right."

153

"And, I told you, I was with Steve the next morning. He certainly wasn't in pain when I last saw him. He was as sharp as ever."

"Making snide suggestions," Craig reminded me. "Implying that there's someone here who wouldn't qualify for a good citizenship medal. And he talked about foxglove, talked about being anxious to meet me, because I'd be curious." Craig reached out to take my hand, pressing it between his palms. "Terry, I don't have another thing to go on; but from what you've told me, I'm convinced that Galvez had something to tell me. And that someone had reason to quiet him."

He was saying that one of the occupants of the rooms down the hall was an attempted murderer! I shuddered, remembering that Denise's door had been unlocked all night. And near dawn . . .

"What about the cat?" I wondered aloud. "I'm almost sure I heard Rudi in this corridor just before Denise screamed."

"You probably did," Craig said. "My guess is that he didn't want to dig up that other kitten at an hour when his sister was liable to catch him in the act. By the time he got around to it, I had already done the job. So, not being terribly bright, he very obligingly provided a substitute; probably some stray cat

154

he found around the place. And, incidentally, this specimen he did strangle. Broke its neck, too, in the process. But he *did* deliver."

"But why would he have put it into Denise's room?" I asked.

"I repeat; he's not exceptionally bright," Craig reminded me. "My room's next door to Denise's. It was an understandable mistake for someone who doesn't come upstairs often."

It was almost too much for me. I was too exhausted and too unnerved for more conjecturing. Certainly I was too bewildered to mention my queasy feeling about Anita Alma. She had quarreled with Steve the night before his departure. She felt rejected by Steve, and she owed him money she was in no position to repay. She had actually threatened him. And, this morning, assuming that she didn't wear false eyelashes and lipstick to bed, she had been wide awake and smartly groomed for a visit to Denise's room. Why?

I didn't ask the question of Craig. He kissed me a few seconds later and I returned to my vigil at Denise's bedside. I had no way of knowing whether Craig's suspicions were purely imaginary. It didn't matter. My own fearful intuition told me not to let Denise out of my sight again, to keep the door locked and . . . what else?

155

Steve's words came to me in the deathly stillness of the room in which my patient slept away the morning: "I would, if I were you, prepare all of Denise's meals myself. This may impose a burden upon you, Terry. However, until you decide to leave this place – and I am certain that you will – you will be wise to draw even the water Denise drinks directly from the tap."

FIFTEEN

Early the next morning, Craig took his grisly package to Dr. Rivera's office for autopsy, leaving me with instructions not to let Denise out of my sight.

Craig's words of caution were unnecessary, of course; I had no intention of exposing our patient to the possibility of another frightening experience. Yet it was difficult to stay with her, and at the same time prepare her meals personally. Only when Van Stuart came to call, at around noon, was I able to go down to the kitchen.

"Please don't leave until I come back with Denise's lunch tray," I whispered to Van.

He shot me a look of bewilderment, but

I was assured that he had no intention of leaving until his departure was demanded.

In the kitchen I found Ilse Westlake instructing the new cook in the art of preparing lobster Thermidor. "Ach, this is such a burden for you, Terry," she insisted. "I will have Belen carry a tray up for the two of you. And I have been wanting to visit with Denise myself. Is she better?"

"She's always fine when Van comes to visit," I said.

Ilse smiled her indulgence. "How quickly the young recover, no? Still, what a terrible shock for the child. I cannot imagine what possessed Rudi." She sighed. "There are times when I wonder if I am doing the right thing . . . if it would not be wiser if he were sent to an institution." Tears welled in her eyes, and I wished that I could tell her that at least part of Rudi's act was not without reason; in his own moronic way he had been responding to a request, and he had mistaken one door for another.

I managed to convince Ilse that I didn't mind fixing the noonday meal for Denise and for myself. Then, as I started out of the kitchen with my tray, I noticed that Ilse was looking out of the rear windows into the garden, her brow wrinkled with confusion.

"Is something wrong?" I asked.

"Durward," she muttered. "He seems more distracted than usual these past few days. He drives himself so hard with his studies. Working so many hours, straining his eyes and his mind." Ilse sighed again and shook her head disconsolately. "Rudi . . . Denise . . . my husband. One worry follows another."

I followed her gaze to where Durward, with his head bowed, and his lanky arms locked behind him in a Napoleonic pose, stood rearranging a fresh mound of soil with the toe of one shoe. If he had known that Denise's kitten had been buried in that spot, he knew, also, that it was no longer there. I felt a chill run through my body. Why was he there? If his behavior had become worrisome to Ilse, who was no stranger to eccentricities, what had caused the change? Was he wondering how his friend was faring in Barcelona?

I learned the answer to that question myself when Craig returned to the castle soon afterward. While Van and Denise chatted, happily ignoring our presence in a corner of the room, Craig whispered a dismal report about Steve:

"Dr. Rivera couldn't reach the doctors he wanted, but he talked to someone at the hospital. It doesn't look encouraging, Terry."

"Is he still on the critical list?"

Craig nodded solemnly. "It's brutal. Unless he's kept under heavy sedation, the pain is unbearable. Cramps, intense thirst, and delirium. He alternates between violent seizures and prostration, and his body is chilled."

I closed my eyes for a moment, empathizing with Steve's misery. "Does that sound like cirrhosis of the liver to you, Craig?"

"It didn't sound like it to Dr. Rivera. He asked if there was a tightening of the skin – if the patient's eyes appeared sunken and sightless. The kind of questions one would ask if poisoning were suspected. Unfortunately, he wasn't speaking to anyone in a position to give him details."

"But he ... you think he suspected poisoning?"

Craig glanced toward Denise and Van, satisfying himself that they weren't listening to our conversation. "I imagine it would have occurred to old Rivera, even if he hadn't phoned for that report. Colleagues don't come into his office every day asking him to do a veterinarian's job."

I had almost forgotten about the autopsy on

159

the Siamese. "What happened there?"

"Evidently I was off base," Craig said. "No toxic material in the stomach or intestines. Neither of us could say for certain what killed the thing, but . . . let's just say no one used it as a mushroom-testing laboratory." Craig was thoughtful for a few seconds. Then, in a reflective tone, he said, "Rivera's an odd character. I couldn't pin him down to any specific opinions. What's more, he seemed to be cautiously avoiding questions that would pinpoint any possible suspicions on my part. He just went about dissecting that kitten's remains as though I had made a perfectly natural request. I imagine his background explains it. When a man's lived in an atmosphere of intrigue and distrust, never knowing whether he was talking to a friend or an enemy, it's logical that he'd become noncommittal. Unless he was sure of his facts and sure of the person who might . . . just *might* share his suspicions."

"Do you think he has them?" I asked.

"Suspicions?" Craig paused. "I know one thing. He told me he was going to keep calling the hospital until he reached Steve's doctors. Because he wanted to ask if the patient was being given glucose."

I frowned. "What would that prove?"

"A low sugar level is a symptom in some

160

types of poisoning."

"Did you question him about that?" I asked.

"Look, Terry, you can't expect two doctors to confer openly about a course of treatment for a patient they haven't examined – a patient under the care of other, presumably qualified physicians. We were sparring around on tenuous grounds. Anything more direct would have amounted to an accusation." Craig was silent again, conscious of a lull in the conversation at the other end of the room. When he spoke again, his words were barely audible. "Can you and Denise be ready to leave tomorrow morning?"

I must have reacted with a startled expression, because Craig explained, "No, we aren't going back to the States. At least, not yet. If anyone asks, we're taking Denise to a heart specialist in Madrid. Dr. Rivera phoned the airport in Palma to make our plane reservations."

"If anyone asks . . . ?"

"I'd rather no one knew this except Rivera," Craig confided. "We aren't going to Madrid. We'll see a cardiac man, but we're going to stop at a hospital, too. And we're only going as far as Barcelona."

SIXTEEN

If our mission had been less grim, Craig and I might have debated whether Palma, with its golden-hazed cathedral rising from masses of purple, crimson, and orange flowering vines, was a more breathtaking sight from the air than the green hill-framed amphitheater of Barcelona, which came into view less than an hour after our plane had left from Majorca.

It would have been a hopeless controversy, but an enjoyable one, like that of gem collectors debating the merits of two flawless, beautiful jewels, or horticulturists lauding the perfection of one rose while comparing it with another, equally lovely.

Only Denise, who remained blissfully unaware of our gloomy thoughts, fully appreciated the sparkling blue expanse of Mediterranean waters below us, the first sight of Barcelona's imposing Gothic spires, or the superb pattern of its modern sector, crisscrossed by graceful avenues and appearing, from the air, like an architect's scale model of the ideally planned city.

"It's like looking at yesterday and tomorrow at the same time," Denise said with her typical enthusiasm. "I'll be glad when this ticker expert gets it across to you two worry-warts that there's nothing wrong with me. Then, maybe we can go sightseeing, huh? I mean, Barcelona dates back to the second century B.C., and it's just *crammed* with fabulous castles and churches and museums and stuff."

Normally, Denise's jargon and uncontained exuberance would have brought an amused smile to Craig's face. Now he merely murmured something about coming back to sightsee at a more convenient time. For it was true that we had not come as tourists. Minutes after our plane touched the ground, instead of visiting architectural wonders that covered a wide span of centuries and encompassed myriad cultures, we were in a hospital so modern that we might almost have been in the New York facility that had brought the three of us together.

Denise was left in the care of a cardiologist recommended by Dr. Rivera. When Craig had acquainted this elderly heart specialist with every detail of the case, and Denise had been ushered into the room where preliminary tests would be made, an elevator took Craig and me to another floor of the hospital.

It was here, at the nurses' station, that a cherub-faced young nun listened attentively as I explained, *"Estamos amigos del señor*

Galvez. Esteban Galvez."

Was my Spanish so hopeless that she hadn't understood that we were Steve's friends? The nun looked from my face to Craig's and then back to me again, with what I took for a lack of comprehension.

"Señor Galvez," Craig repeated.

"Sí, Señores, comprendo," the little nun replied softly. It was then that I realized that her expression was not one of bewilderment, but of compassion. *"Lo siento mucho, señores."* She spoke in the hushed, respectful tone that every doctor or nurse is obliged to use at times. And she was telling us she was sorry. *"El señor Galvez – pobrecito, se murio a las ocho y media este mañana."*

I felt chilled suddenly, as though a cold wind had shuddered past me. It seemed incredible that Steve was dead, that the long days and nights of suffering had been senseless, that we had arrived too late! Too late for what? To help him? He had died at eight thirty this morning in spite of the efforts of medical people who were no doubt as dedicated to saving his life as Craig and I would have been. Too late to help him? Or to hear him name his murderer?

I remember Craig leading me to a settee in the reception room. Assured that although I was stunned I was *not* going to faint, he excused himself to go in search of someone with whom he could communicate – someone who would know the details of Steve's case.

During Craig's absence, the soft-spoken nun, a member of a nursing order, brought me a glass of water and managed to tell me that she had been present when the unfortunate Señor Galvez had expired. From what I understood, the patient had welcomed death. Death had come as a desperately craved blessing; I deduced that I was being asked to take comfort in that thought.

Catching only about half of the commiserations and condolences, I remained bound up in my own jumbled thoughts. Then, gradually, it became clear to me that the nun was wondering if I might be the Parisian sweetheart Señor Galvez had called for in his delirium. The Senor's aunt, now prostrated by grief, had wondered, too, about the identity of this loved one. For, between spasms, repeatedly, Esteban Galvez had cried, *"Ella . . . ella! Amita!"*

"She . . . she! Little sweetheart!" I repeated Steve's deathbed sentence to Craig late that afternoon, as a taxi swept us away from the hospital and into Barcelona's late-afternoon traffic. "I can't imagine Steve referring to any woman as his 'little sweetheart,' " I added.

"Not even a woman he might have loved."

"He was either drugged or crazed by pain from the time he was brought to the hospital," Craig reminded me. "The man was delirious . . . he could have said anything."

I agreed, yet the phrase continued to haunt me. It would have been unthinkable for strangers, especially inarticulate strangers, to call on Steve's Aunt Victoria at a time when she was despondent over the loss of her only relative. Still, I wished that I could verify those puzzling words. "She . . . she . . . *amita!*" Besides, meeting the old woman would create unpleasant complications; could we tell her that we had met her beloved nephew in Majorca . . . expose a dead man's lie about attending university classes in Paris?

Craig's voice stirred me out of my thoughts. "Denise was surprisingly cooperative about staying overnight," he was saying. "We want to be certain, but from present indications, her heart's perfectly sound. Do you know what that says to me, Terry?"

"That her heart seizure was induced," I guessed.

"If Dr. Rivera's charts are correct – and I have every reason to believe they are – Denise suffered *more* than one cardiac irregularity. To me, that means she was given more than one

166

carefully measured dose of digitalis, probably in its raw state."

I had been waiting for Craig to tell me what he had learned from Steve's doctors; he had been in conference with the medical team for the better part of an hour. Now, he revealed that he was less positive about the circumstances surrounding Steve's death than those that had affected Denise. "The doctors never discounted the possibility of poisoning," he told me. "But when I asked them if mushroom poisoning had been considered they became understandably touchy. After all, I had nothing more scientific than a hunch to go on, and they *had* run an analysis of the stomach contents. They found nothing toxic, nothing to support my second-guessing theory. I had the feeling that they were being excessively polite to an upstart who was questioning their competence."

Craig stared out at the broad cypress-lined avenue for a few moments, apparently re-experiencing the unpleasant interview. Then he said, "One of the doctors told me that the only mushroom capable of producing such violent symptoms would have been – what did he say – out of the question in this case. Otherwise, he said, he would certainly have administered a known anti-toxin."

"If your . . . guess had been right, would

that have saved Steve?" I asked. "Did the doctor think . . . ?"

"He said it might have given the patient a fifty-fifty chance of survival. *If* it had been administered immediately. Ethically, I was on the shakiest ground imaginable, Terry. I was wrong about the kitten, too, remember? And yet Rivera had asked those pointed questions on the phone – asking about specific symptoms." Craig ran an unsteady hand over his forehead. "I can't help thinking those doctors aren't satisfied. Still, they weren't going to tell a total stranger, a foreign doctor, that they'd made a wrong diagnosis. I would have understood; I know what it means to be baffled by a medical mystery. But they had no reason to trust me with their self-doubt. And I'll *swear* they were in doubt, Terry. The way they glanced at each other when I mentioned mushrooms . . ."

As our taxi rounded a circular parkway, two isolated thoughts struck me with the blinding force of lightning bolts. One flash, and then another! "Craig, they admitted there *was* a mushroom capable of killing Steve in that manner. When they said it was impossible that he'd consumed it, what were their facts? That the mushroom isn't in season at this time of the year? In Paris? Or in Barcelona? They couldn't have known that Steve had just come from a castle in Majorca, where anything can be raised at any time because —"

"Because there's a mycologist tending the spawn in a hothouse!" Craig exclaimed. He leaned forward, directing the driver to take us to a bookstore. When he settled back in the seat beside me, he said, "We'd probably find what we need on Durward's shelves, but this will be less risky. If we find a volume on mushrooms, we'll get someone to translate anything we can't decipher for ourselves. Without tipping our hand to Durward."

"It's not Durward I'm afraid of," I whispered. "Craig, think! *'Ella ... ella ... Amita!'* It doesn't seem logical that Steve wouldn't have recognized poisonous mushrooms. If he *had* eaten them, I imagine he'd have gotten sick immediately. So maybe we've been on the wrong track. Suppose there *was* some poison that could have been gotten to him later — after he left the castle. I don't know what or how, but suppose he remembered who had threatened his life? She! It was a woman. A woman who had said, 'You will writhe in agony for your sins against me.' Even when he was in agony, Steve would have realized what had happened. He would have tried to name that 'she,' Craig."

"I don't follow you."

"He was probably only half coherent. The

169

nurse and his aunt might have misunderstood him." I paused for breath as the cab driver swung around in a U-turn, reversing our direction. "He wasn't saying 'little sweetheart' – *amita*. He was trying to tell someone –"

"*Anita!*" Craig muttered under his breath.

"She despised Walter Westlake for rejecting her," I went on. "She could have learned about the effects of foxglove in Durward's library."

Craig's mind was racing along with mine. "It seems so obvious now! The markings in that book! Durward wouldn't have had to check on information that elementary. And he called the book a priceless collector's item. No book collector would make ink marks in a rare volume. Only an amateur seeking information would have defaced those pages!"

"All right, suppose she had intended to kill Denise, and the dosage wasn't strong enough?" I conjectured.

"Why? The motive seems so flimsy."

"She may be psychotic. Possessed with an urge to get back at men who don't want her. Let's assume that she tried to get back at Walter by killing his daughter. Assume that Steve figured out what had happened. He hinted at it. He played cat and mouse with her, and he made it clear that he was going to talk to *you* about it. Anita couldn't have taken that chance. Besides, Steve had treated her like vermin. Embarrassed her, ridiculed her." The final motive suggested itself in almost the same breath: "And she owed him money, Craig. They had a bitter argument about that."

Craig sat quietly for a time, absorbing this new line of reasoning. When he had weighed all the implications long enough, he said, "There isn't one shred of even circumstantial evidence, Terry. We could pile up a mountain of motives, but we're still only guessing. No poison in the man's digestive system, every indication that he left Majorca in good health and, from what the doctors told me, *remained* in good health for nearly two days afterward. You can't crucify a woman because she's frustrated. Not even when she's made threats."

Craig was right. There was no ground on which to accuse Anita Alma of murder except a possibly misunderstood word . . . the dying utterance of a pain-crazed man.

Nor was there hope that our questions about Steve's death would be answered by an autopsy. "Without admitting to Steve's aunt that they were wrong in their preliminary diagnosis, the doctors can't ask for a postmortem," Craig said. "From what I've heard of the woman, she'd take a dim view of letting a pathologist cut her nephew's body open. Not unless someone convinced her that Steve *had* been murdered. And who's going to approach the old lady with that?"

A fading sun had transformed the medieval palace on our right into a structure of shimmering gold. In spite of the city's ethereal beauty, we were silent and glum as our driver steered us toward the bookshop. Were Craig's thoughts paralleling mine?

The burned letter, the dead cats, Steve's incriminating remarks, Denise's sudden illness. Steve's ghastly death. *Amita* ... *Anita. She!* None of it made sense! There was nothing to cling to but a series of tenuous threads, threads that snapped when an attempt was made to weave them together. Yet, somehow, these ghostly strands persisted in dangling over our heads, defying us to spin from them a tapestry made of sterner fabric than suspicion.

The threads were tightened a short time later in a musty shop over which hung an ornately lettered sign proclaiming LIBROS.

It was Craig who found the needed volume – a prosaic-looking textbook for students of mycology. As we thumbed through the book, I was the one who spotted a chapter heading that screamed out a shocking new clue. And it was the wizened old bibliophile shopkeeper who obliged us with a translation of the brief chapter in question.

When we left the shop, instructing our driver to take us to the airport, we did not know who had made the attempt on Denise's life. Nor did we know who had subjected Esteban Galvez to his inhumanly cruel death. But we *did* know that Steve had not named his murderer.

Wracked by an agony that the book described as "unendurable," Steve had remained enigmatic to the end. He had only hinted at the identity of the killer. Or perhaps he, himself, was uncertain of who and why. But he had been explicit in explaining *how*.

The final keys to the puzzle waited for us at Castillo de los Tres Gatos, keys that would tell us whether Steve's dying word had actually been not *"amita,"* not "Anita," but a word with which Durward Westlake would be completely familiar: *Amanita, Amanita phalloides!*

SEVENTEEN

Perhaps the guilt for Steve's murder, or the very fact that he *had* been murdered, would never have been established if a temperamental new cook named Belen Tirado had not become angered by Anita Alma's imperious behavior.

Certainly the plan that Craig and I had discussed during our flight to Majorca would have been delayed. As it happened, Ilse Westlake was in a swivet when we arrived at the castle.

"At least there is *some* good news," she said when Craig gave her the preliminary report on Denise. "It is a relief to know that I can stop worrying about the child. Ach, it is not enough to worry about one's family. I must be driven to distraction by servants and houseguests as well!"

I winced at the mention of worrying about houseguests; had she learned that Steve had been hospitalized?

Apparently not. "I have just wasted hours of my precious time training the new cook. And at noon today, what do you suppose, Terry? Belen carries to Anita her breakfast tray. Anita is suffering from a hangover and she complains that the coffee is not hot enough." Ilse demonstrated the cook's reaction by pretending to grab a tray out of my hands and slamming it to the floor. *This* is what Belen gives for an answer. And in spite of my attempts to pacify the woman, she announces that she will no longer be abused by 'drunken foreigners who sleep away the morning and treat decent folk like cattle.' "

A wave of hope rose up inside me. "And Belen quit?"

"Walked out the door as high and mighty as a queen." Ilse sighed. "Leaving me to worry about a dinner party for twelve tomorrow night. To say nothing of our dinner this evening."

It was as though the situation had been made to order. "Let me fix dinner," I offered. "I love to cook, you know. With Denise gone, I'll have time on my hands tonight."

Ilse protested that I must be tired. "I know you did not realize Denise would be detained overnight, and you were not prepared to stay. To Madrid and back in so short a time! No, no, you are too exhausted." Ilse patted my shoulder, and in a laughing, confidential tone, she added, "Since Anita's bad temper is to blame, we will let her ladyship serve us dinner, yes? Although I will admit my good friend would not create any sensations at the Cordon Bleu!"

"I'm a whiz at Spaghetti alla Romano," I said. "Let me do the honors, Ilse. Please?"

Fortunately, Ilse gave in to my pressure. "Perfect," Craig said when I reported my success.

We had deliberately stalled in Palma for several hours; long enough to make our purported trip to Madrid seem feasible. While there, we had made a simple purchase. Craig hurried out to his rented car now to fetch that package. With the contents, we baited our hook for a killer.

There were six of us at the table. Besides Craig and myself, there were the Westlakes, of course, and Anita, looking ravishing in a sheath dress of white raw silk, and in spite of the fact that her heavy makeup somehow failed to conceal telltale lines of dissipation under her eyes. Our sextet was completed by Rudi Gerhardt; since Steve's departure, and oblivious to Anita's distaste, Ilse had taken to allowing her brother to sit at the dinner table when no outside guests were invited.

A gay atmosphere prevailed, reminiscent of Steve's last night at the castle. It was difficult for me to play my role as the carefree amateur chef, happily accepting the compliments of the diners; my thoughts reverted again and again to the last time we had gathered in this informal fashion. Steve Galvez had been part of the hilarity, then. Had one of the people at this table known that he would soon be writhing in mortal agony?

Steve had contributed a choice wine for

that occasion. This night, the wine had been provided by our host, and once again he proposed a toast to Denise's good health. "To Denise," Durward said. "But, more so, to Dr. Addison, who has finally put an end to all the ridiculous distractions revolving around her . . . delicate condition."

Ilse laughed. "You see how naive my dear husband is? Delicate condition, Durward, is a euphemism we can hardly apply to our niece."

Durward shrugged his indifference and everyone drank. We ate in silence for a few minutes after that, and then Anita said, "I propose another toast." She held up her wineglass and nodded at me. "To Terecita, an infinitely better cook than that madwoman who did us the favor of removing her presence this afternoon. Terry not only does not hurl crockery at people who have splitting headaches, but she prepares the most divine Italian food this side of Firenze."

Surprisingly, Durward, who rarely commented on the food, agreed. "Excellent, Terry."

Rudi responded by stuffing another forkful into his misshapen mouth, a not wholly successful maneuver that brought a pained expression to his sister's face.

"I only wish Terry had saved her talent for

our guests tomorrow night," Ilse said. Her next comment served as the cue Craig had been waiting for: "I had always been told Americans cook with their can openers. How did anyone raised in the United States manage to make such a delicious sauce?"

"The secret's in the mushrooms, I think," Craig said casually. He turned to me and feigned a mischievous grin. "I still insist that old crone you bought them from is a witch."

"Oh, she was just a poor little peasant woman," I said "She'd once worked as a maid for a Boston family living in Palma, she told me. Picked up a surprising amount of English."

"If she *was* a witch," Durward said, "she probably thought you were a member of an American coven, out buying supplies. I suppose, knowing you're an American, she offered to sell you instant mandrake root?"

"What a way to talk about a superb cook!" Ilse protested. "I believe you're jealous, Durward."

"Not jealous, cautious," Durward quipped. "If Terry's been dealing with witches, my dear friends, we may all be dining on pasta flavored with *Amanita phalloides*." He chuckled at his own joke and refilled his plate from the silver serving dish at his side.

I glanced across the table at Craig. *Now*, his

eyes told me. *Now!*

"That *was* the name she used," I said, pretending complete innocence. "She said she's been picking the same mushrooms out in the countryside for years, and someone apparently told her the Latin name for them."

Durward laughed aloud this time. "Someone told her wrong, old girl. *Amanita phalloides*, indeed!"

"Terry's right," Craig said. "That's the name the old woman used."

Durward shook his head in disparagement. "Understand, I'm not doubting the woman's peasant knowledge of fungi. I'd trust an old Majorcan vendor to know the difference between ... say, a delectable St. George's mushroom and a highly poisonous leaden entoloma, before I'd trust a professor of mycology. This, in spite of the fact that the two look almost identical – even to the practiced eye. The point I'm trying to make is that, when the scholarly expert doubled up with cramps after eating one of the damned things, *he'd* know that he'd mistaken an *Entoloma lividum* for a *Calocybe gambora*. You see, I have unbounded faith in your old lady's *empirical* knowledge, Terry. I merely take issue with her scientific terminology."

I continued my ignorant pose, aware that the others were engrossed in the conversation.

"Well, she *could* have been right. She seemed very sure of herself."

"If she knew what she was saying, which I'm inclined to doubt, the old creature was pulling your leg," Durward insisted. "A time-honored sport among natives who deal with tourists. You see, Terry, the *Amanita phalloides* is popularly known as the Death Cap, and it's the deadliest fungus known to man. It contains three distinct, virulent poisons, the most potent of which is amanatin. Why, in laboratory tests, a dose of five-millionths of a gram has been known to kill a mouse. A single slice will kill a human being – under exceedingly unpleasant circumstances, I might add. And in spite of an antitoxin development at the Pasteur Institute, the mortality rate exceeds fifty-five percent." Durward winked at me facetiously. "I presume your sister-witch told you that there is no true antidote known?"

"Must we discuss gruesome matters at the table?" Anita complained. "If I had known you were going to start on one of your disgusting lectures, Durward, I would never have mentioned Terry's genius as a cook." She turned toward me, changing the subject abruptly, returning the conversation to its original course. "Did you study cooking as part of your nurse's training, Terry? The fields *are* rather related, are they not?" Her patronizing manner announced that she equated R.N.'s with the lowliest of servants. Her glance at Craig assured him that she was democratically kind to the kitchen help, providing they kept their place.

Durward, once launched on a favorite subject, was not easily dissuaded. Everything he had said up to that point had been verified by the book Craig and I had purchased in Barcelona, but now, ignoring Anita, he added a clinching, personal opinion to his argument: "These local peasants delight in making fools of green foreigners. If your old crone knew what the *Amanita phalloides* is, she was having a good laugh at your expense. Rest assured, however, that she knew what she was picking. She certainly wouldn't have been selling amanitas in the marketplace!"

Craig set his fork aside, frowning. "I don't know," he said slowly. "She was an old one. Malevolent sort of character. She..." He looked at me with a questioning expression. "She could have been psychotic, Terry. That insane cackle ... remember? She could have been completely mad."

"Mad or not," Durward said wearily, "she presents no threat to anyone who enjoys your spaghetti sauce, dear girl. At least not for several months. The Death Cap doesn't appear until midsummer – often not until the end of autumn."

In spite of Durward's joking dismissal, an electric tension crackled around the table. "It . . . could be cultivated," Ilse said. She was staring into her dinner plate, her round face suddenly drained of its rosy color.

Rudi had said nothing until then. Now he pointed his fork at Durward. "You grow some in little tray, *ja?*"

"Of course I did," Durward said irritably. "To photograph. For use in illustrating my book. But I'm sure no one else would trouble to locate the spores and raise the vicious things."

"A . . . psychotic person might," Ilse said. Her voice was a dry whisper. "Craig said this woman acted crazy."

Craig and I exchanged darting glances; Ilse had laid aside her fork and was gazing at the serving dish with an expression of undisguised terror.

Anita's musical laugh rippled from her throat. "Oh, this morbid talk! It's ridiculous! Really, Ilse, if our new cook had been trading with a mad witch, I am sure we would all be out of our misery by this time. Besides, we have taste buds, no? I am not one to ruin my figure with second helpings . . . eating some vile-tasting poison."

182

"That's not true." Ilse choked. "The mushroom has an excellent flavor. There is no disagreeable odor. If there were only a few bits of the *Amanita phalloides* mixed in with the common field mushroom, we wouldn't know it!"

Anita sprinkled the remainder of her portion with parmesan cheese. "I just said we would know it by *now*, darling."

"No, no! Amanatin works slowly!" Ilse pushed her plate forward and rose to her feet, backing away from the table as though from an attacking cobra. "It may be as long as forty hours before the poison takes effect." Panic-stricken, she looked from Craig to Durward, inviting their corroboration. "That is true, it is not? By the time the symptoms appear, the poison is no longer in the stomach. It is in the blood stream ... and *there is no antidote!*"

Ilse's voice had risen to a strident, hysterical pitch, and Rudi got up to grasp her forearm with his crippled hand. Clinging to his sister like a frightened child, he whimpered, "The little cat no die slow. I going die slow? Not give little cat same poison as here?"

Ilse shook herself free of him in a violent motion, hissing, "Be still, you babbling idiot!"

Rudi made the gurgling sound of a

wounded animal, covering his face with his hands.

"This is . . . unfortunate," Ilse said. She was breathing heavily, her lips trembling. "I should not have . . . become upset." She made a shrill attempt at laughter. "My nerves . . . my wild imagination. How silly of me. We must serve the dessert, Terry. Such a . . . lovely dessert!" She lowered herself to her chair, fighting for composure.

"Your irrational behavior depresses me," Durward said quietly. "However, your knowledge astounds me, Ilse." He remained motionless, eyeing his wife with the detached interest of a scientist. "I shouldn't have scoffed at Steve when he told me you were beginning to take a genuine interest in my work."

"I? An interest?" Ilse's hand fluttered in disagreement. "Ach, I will never understand those complicated scientific . . ."

"You know what digitalis does to the heart, don't you, Mrs. Westlake?" Craig was standing now, his eyes fixed unwaveringly on Ilse's face.

"But that is absurd!" Ilse cried. "Who told you this? Esteban! Steve! He told you lies about me! When did you see him?"

"I saw him this morning," Craig said evenly.

184

Ilse caught an audible breath. Blood drained from her face, and her watery eyes bulged with a mingled terror and fury. "You went to the hospital to spy on me! I knew you were not gone long enough to go to Madrid! He sent for you and you believed his lies! I suppose he told you I was responsible for his condition! Durward . . . Anita . . . you *know* how he lies! I had nothing to do with –"

"What condition?" Craig persisted. "What condition do you mean, Mrs. Westlake?"

It was like seeing a human being disintegrate before our eyes. "I did not mean –" Ilse sputtered. She began again. "That is, I thought, since you had gone to a hospital . . . you might have . . . if Steve was in the hospital, there must have been *something* wrong with him, but I swear – I swear that whatever he told you, I am completely innocent! Someone else must have tried to kill him. I know nothing! I – stop staring at me, all of you! What reason would I have to poison Steve?"

I added the final barb to Craig's inquisition: "How did you know that Steve was poisoned, Ilse?"

Anita gasped. "Oh, no! No, you must be wrong! Esteban . . . oh, my poor darling! Why did you not tell me he is ill?"

"I'm sorry," Craig said. He kept his eyes

185

on Ilse's face. "There was only one way to learn who murdered him."

There was a stricken cry from Anita before she dropped her head to the table. *"Esteban! No, no!"*

Rudi threw his arms around Ilse and released a spine-chilling howl. Only Durward retained his calm. Ilse had leaped to her feet again and was shrieking like a banshee:

"I will admit nothing! So he is dead – all to the good; he will not be able to lie about me again. I know nothing about the foxglove. My husband is the one who knows of such things. It was Durward who prepared that dinner, not I. You were all in the kitchen. Any of you could have dropped a handful of the poisonous mushrooms into Steve's omelet. Who will believe you? *You!"* Ilse looked around at the table wildly and then made a diving motion to grasp a murderous bread knife. "You, with your honeyed manners, listening to Steve tormenting me . . . lying, lying . . ."

She lunged at me blindly, slashing out with the serrated knife as Craig leaped up to grab her arm. The blade flashed for an instant in the candlelight and then, as Rudi's weight threw her aim off balance, the glittering steel was no longer visible. There was a gutteral sound from Rudi – a horrible, bubbling sound

186

that stilled Ilse's insane tirade. For a frozen eternity all of us stood locked in a motionless tableau, watching the crimson stain rise below Rudi's shoulderblade, where the imbedded knife still quivered like a dying bird. Then, like a puppet whose strings have been cut, Rudi's powerful arm loosened its grip around Ilse and the grotesque body slid to the floor. As he dropped, his maimed hand brushed the edge of the table, flaccid and lifeless.

Ilse's scream died in her throat. She made no move, looking on with a painted mask of horror as Craig bent over Rudi's body. A minute later, Craig looked up to tell us that the nightmare of Rudi Gerhardt's existence was ended.

Still later, we drove an immobile, blankly staring Ilse to the authorities in Palma. Durward stayed behind, explaining that more urgent matters called him back to his study.

EIGHTEEN

Rudi Gerhardt's incongruous death, as senseless and cruel as his life had been, crumbled Ilse's defenses completely. Not only was she completely unnerved, but apparently

187

the police authorities who questioned her were more skilled than Craig and I had been. Besides, their probing was backed by more than mere suspicion of murder; within two days their investigation was spurred by an autopsy report from Barcelona.

Perhaps Ilse realized that her blundering denials at the dinner table had been, in effect, a confession of murder before four witnesses. When she broke, her story gushed forth from her lips in every minute detail.

Seeing Denise's illness as a golden opportunity, Ilse had hoped to build up a medically authenticated case of cardiac irregularity in her niece. Walter Westlake could not go on bucking his doctor's advice for long without bringing on a fatal heart attack. With Walter dead, a second "heart attack" on the part of his daughter would not be suspect. In the unlikely event that "stupid old Rivera" would detect the use of digitalis, Ilse's supposed ignorance of drugs found in the garden would focus the spotlight of guilt on the poisonous plant expert, Durward.

Ilse's plans were proceeding so smoothly that she was even able to convert setbacks to assets. When I discovered that my letter to Craig Addison had been destroyed, it was easy to shift the blame; while she was apologizing for Rudi, she knew that I remained suspicious of Durward. It was a form of insurance that Ilse took advantage of, in the unlikely event that someone might question Denise's final "heart attack." If the murder charge arose, Durward would be disposed of, freeing Ilse to pursue the glittering social life that was an obsession with her. Walter Westlake's advertising fortune would free ner from the constant scrimping that now frustrated her dream of being hostess to the Continental elite.

She had not taken Steve Galvez into account. He was clever and observing, a shrewd judge of unscrupulous character, since his own love of luxury involved occasional deceit. Steve recognized Denise's symptoms immediately after her collapse at the fiesta and guessed why and by whom the foxglove potion had been brewed. He discovered Ilse's source of information, the ancient herbal encyclopedia in Durward's library. He, too, had known that the ink marks had been made by someone who cared little about priceless books and was a neophyte in the use of drug plants.

Instead of facing Ilse with his discovery directly, Steven enjoyed the process of needling her. He made deliberate references to foxglove, and the other plants Ilse had checked, for possible future use. He dropped sly innuendoes that frightened Ilse, and let it be known that he intended to tell Denise's doctor why the girl appeared in good health one day and suffered cardiac irregularity the next. It was clear to Ilse that the sardonic Spaniard would have to be silenced.

To her delight, Ilse's secretive research disclosed a means by which Steve could be given a poison that would not take effect until he was far from the scene of the crime. By the time it took effect it would be undetectable and uncontrollable.

How perfectly everything fell into place! Durward was in the process of raising the Death Caps at a time when they were not in season; no doctor would dream that Steve had consumed the vicious poison. The early symptoms, such as a hardening of the liver, were similar to those of a disease Steve had been tempting with alcohol throughout his adult life. And to make the scheme completely foolproof, if it *were* discovered that he had been poisoned, no one would trace him to the Castillo de los Tres Gatos; by his own admission, he had spent the past few months in Paris.

Even beyond that, should murder be suspected and an accusation brought to the castle doorstep, who would be suspected? A naive woman whose life revolved around dinner parties, or a man who knew all there was to know about the use of the ghastly things he raised in his hothouse?

Ilse's test on the Siamese kitten had been a qualified success; the onset and the death had been strangely sudden. Too strong a dose, Ilse had decided. Accordingly, into the omelet Durward was preparing for Steve, she had dropped only a few slices of the mushroom obtained from the hothouse. The amanita had been indistinguishable from the *Agaricus campestris* already folded into the mixture. In that single surreptitious motion, Ilse had not only assured herself of a future fortune, but as an added bonus, she had wiped out a current debt. Or so she had believed.

"What we don't know," I said to Craig while he watched me pack Denise's clothes for the trip home, "and what Ilse didn't tell the police, is why Rudi killed that other cat and brought it to this room."

"I don't imagine Rudi did anything without first getting his sister's approval," Craig guessed. "He must have told her that I had asked him to exhume the Siamese. Maybe she suggested the substitute. Or maybe, when Rudi discovered that I had already dug up the kitten I wanted, he obligingly provided his own pet. Maybe you're right, honey. We aren't ever going to know."

An unnatural silence hung over the castle. Terrified by the events, the two maids had departed. Not only were they unlikely to return, but it was a safe bet that their awesome tales of intrigue, murder, and bloody violence would revive among the villagers their traditional dread of this sepulcher on the mountainside; not one of the superstitious inhabitants of San Ysidro would ever be induced to venture up the castle road again.

Anita Alma, too, was gone. Having given her testimony to the authorities, she would not return to this area until she was called as a witness in Ilse Westlake's trial. I had been amazed by the genuineness of her grief over Steve's death; perhaps I had not understood the bond that existed between these two unproductive, dissipated, and worldly-wise cynics. Anita had cried her heart out over a man who had humiliated her at every turn. Was she mourning Esteban Galvez? I wondered. Or did she weep because, in that rootless, constantly searching, luxury-loving parasite, she had caught an accurate glimpse of herself? The bell that had tolled for Steve had brought Anita another day closer to the grave she feared.

We had not brought Denise back to the castle. Once Craig had determined that his patient's only heart problem was a romantic one, he had approved an invitation from Van Stuart's parents, asking Denise to stay at their villa until the "current unpleasantness" was over, and we were ready to go home.

Denise's joy over this turn of events was going a long way to counteract the shock of discovering that her sweet-tempered, overly solicitous aunt was a murderess.

But another thought plagued Denise even more; Steve would not have died his barbarous death if he had not concerned himself with saving life. No one would make her forget that awesome fact, but Van's nearness would lighten any burden for Denise. And he had already announced his intention of enrolling in the same New York university Denise had chosen to attend the following semester.

Now, with almost everyone gone from the castle, the silence had an oppressive quality. I felt as though the somber portraits on the walls might break into that unearthly quiet and speak.

I finished packing the last few items Denise had not required at the Stuarts' villa. My own luggage had already been carried down to Craig's rented car. "It's strange, isn't it, that cats played a role in exposing another murderer in this gloomy place."

Craig had heard the old legend from Ilse herself. "That's true. We might have convinced ourselves that nothing was wrong here if it hadn't been for those two dead kittens. I hope you haven't formed any unpleasant associations, Terry."

"No. I'm like the unfortunate lady who lived here once. I happen to be very fond of cats."

Before we started downstairs, I told Craig about my childhood wish. "I think wanting a kitten was a symbolic thing with me." I concluded. "A pet was ... part and parcel of having a home. A place where you were surrounded by permanent things. Lasting responsibilities. People who –"

"– who loved you?" Craig's arms encircled me gently. "This was what I wanted from marriage, Terry. It took me years to get over my disappointment – years before I stopped fearing that my ideal was an impossible one. I don't like to admit it now, but when I got your cable, I was ... frankly, less concerned about Denise than by the possibility that I might never see you again if I didn't rush to your side immediately." He planted a tender kiss on my forehead. "This isn't the place to talk, darling."

Craig was right. Castillo de los Tres Gatos held too many horrible memories to qualify as a place to discuss plans for a happy future. Now that Denise no longer needed a nurse, I had been happily fired from my job. Denise was a welcome guest with Van's family; Craig had arranged for a month-long absence from his practice. And there was all of Majorca to see, all the loveliness of the other Balearic Islands, all of the romance of Spain.

Craig must have been thinking identical thoughts. "Can you think of a better locale for a honeymoon?" he asked. "Dr. Rivera should be able to give us advice about how and where tourists go to get married. Let's say goodbye to Durward and go."

Durward had rarely emerged from his study since his wife had been taken into police custody. We found him there, seated at his desk, the space before him littered with papers, books and photographs of botanical specimens. He looked more gaunt, more pale than ever. But, pen in hand, he was writing with an intensity that spoke of compressed power.

"We're leaving, Durward," Craig said. "We don't want to disturb you, but we wanted to say goodbye."

Our host did not look up from the paper on which he was making his frenzied inscriptions. Craig looked to me for a way out of the embarrassing snub.

"We'd just like to tell you we're . . . sorry about all that's happened," I said.

Durward nodded impatiently, without interrupting his scribbling.

"We came to say goodbye," Craig repeated.

Durward's response was a vague wave of his left hand. We stood in the doorway for a few moments longer and then retreated from the room, closing the door behind us.

There had been no personal affront intended, we knew. Durward Westlake had only one interest, and in its fanatical pursuit he was protested from both the joys and the miseries of human contact. If he was writing, now, his dissertation on the virulent *Amanita phalloides* mushroom, he was doing it with a scholarly concentration that allowed no room for emotions. That his friend's excruciating death was attributable to the subject of his current study was a secondary matter. That his wife had admitted, murdering one human being, and had planned to murder his brother's only child, had no bearing on the important project before him.

Ironically, and typically, Durward was undisturbed by the fact that Ilse had cold-bloodedly planned to use him as a patsy if the need arose. He was considerably more distressed by the date for which the trial had been set; as a principal witness, he would have his work interrupted at the height of the summer growing season!

Several years have passed since Craig and I closed the door on that dimly lighted study and passed, for the last time, through the musty vestibule of the Castillo. The library and its adjoining hothouse are only dim memories now; the fear and the horror are all but forgotten, except as I have revived them here. And when we recall Majorca, we remember glistening blue bays and flower-lined patios warmed by a friendly sun.

There are new and happy thoughts to occupy us. Although I have not been inside a hospital since Craig, Jr. was born, I am still interested in the medical profession, and I share my husband's concern with his practice. We have our wonderful little son; we have each other. We have our home, and we delight in our friends, among them, Van and Denise Stuart.

We see less of the Stuarts, since we settled in far-separated suburbs, than we see of Walter Westlake. Our conversations with him usually revolve around the work he loves, and his stubborn resistance to Craig's efforts at slowing him down.

In consideration of his health, we avoid disturbing topics. Long ago, Ilse's life sentence closed the doors on the subject of this memoir. Accordingly, we have never asked Walter whether the monthly checks to his brother are still sent to a forbidding gray castle high above San Ysidro.

I think not. More likely the dark and massive door has been locked, the portraits left to mildew on cold, damp walls, the furniture to gather dust. If villagers climb up to the Castillo de los Tres Gatos at all, I daresay they are urchins who have discovered the sport of demolishing small panes of glass with rocks; if any plants remain in the hothouse, they are probably withered and dry.

I think too, that enough time has elapsed for Durward Westlake to have written the last chapter in his cheerless book – as I now complete the final words in mine.

The publishers hope that this book has given you enjoyable reading. Large Print Books are specially designed to be as easy to see and hold as possible. If you wish a complete list of our books, please ask at your local library or write directly to: Curley Publishing, Inc., P.O. Box 37, South Yarmouth, Massachusetts, 02664.